A PLAN TO SAVE
THE WORLD

Elaelah Harley

Chapter One

A sharp intake of breath followed by an impatient gulp. It was a normal reaction to being startled.

Willa swallowed once more as her eyes focused on the spot beyond her beige curtains, eight floors down and into the city. Something had distracted her, and she wasn't distracted easily.

Maybe she should've closed her curtains then. What good has curiosity ever gotten her? Besides, she rarely liked peering over the streets below. The city glow irritated her sleep, and the noise of the train tracks disturbed her dreams. But tonight, she didn't plan to drown out the world so soon. She had an exam the next day – one that prompted a late night of study.

She huffed, looking down at the laptop resting in front of her.

Focus, Willa. Focus.

The flash of light came again, drawing her eyes back to the window. This time, she was sure it wasn't the regular city lights that hid behind her curtains. Her body responded, on alert, her shoulders jolting every time a flood of blue light entered the room. Something was happening down below.

She noted the time on the top corner of her laptop – 11:52pm. Of course, the time wasn't strange. Night owls like herself were probably still awake in their homes. But when it came to her street, this was peculiar. The shops surrounding her apartment would close just after five. Even by eight, apart from the half-hourly train, the area was barren.

Willa looked away once more before seeing the strange blue light flash in the corner of her eye again.

Her resolve snapped. She slammed her laptop shut and jumped off the bed, landing with her face propped against the window, eyes staring widely into the distance.

She kept her gaze at a darkened area of the city – near the train tracks and the outer town centre. After what felt like minutes, she saw the light directly.

The darkened area was home to a tiny spark. One that could be mistaken as a dropped, half-lit cigarette bud until it grew to illuminate the surrounding area.

"Camera flash?" Willa guessed.

The flashes now occurred more regularly. Each time, there was always a small burn before the entire area radiated blue.

To Willa, the flash could have been anything, so she allowed her imagination to run wild with both practical and impractical causes. She focused even harder and saw two figures through the flashes. People.

But what were they doing? Was she seeing something she shouldn't be seeing? Should she be cautious? Maybe she would just sit this one out.

Willa stood up and stretched as she tried to ground herself. When she got caught being nosy as a child, she found stretching relaxed her, taking her mind off the hyper-fixation. It was a bad habit of hers to meddle with the business of others, but one she never learned to shake.

What were they doing? She honestly didn't know. What she knew, however, was that for some reason, she wanted to find out.

Willa loudly barged into her cupboards, pulling out whatever wearable warmth she could find. She grabbed her keys and phone, darkened storefront, Charlie began his spiel of accusation.

"I suppose you liked something in the window… so you shattered the glass to get inside. The shards wounded your hand, and you began running when you saw me."

"Do you even hear yourself right now? That's ridiculous!" Willa rolled her eyes.

He gave her a stern eye. "So, why did you do it?"

"I didn't." Willa looked away, unamused by the reoccurring accusation.

"You know what, maybe I was wrong."

Her eyes filled with hope, and she held her arms up, gesturing for him to free them. "That's what I've been saying!"

"This store doesn't seem like your style. You're clearly interested in something more… casual." His voice took a mocking turn.

She looked down to the winter warmers she'd quickly dressed in. Now he was just being petty.

"Oh, give me a break, Charles," she dropped her hands, realising he wasn't going to free her any time soon.

"And what might your name be?"

"Willa."

"Last name?"

"Triston?" she snapped back, wondering why it mattered.

Charlie reached into his pocket and took out his phone. He dialled a few digits and waited for an answer. "Hey, Joe? Yeah – I'm in the area. I'm going to need a backup car, there's been a break-in. Suspect's name is Willa Triston."

"Are you kidding me?" Willa complained.

"I advise you to keep your mouth shut next time you get arrested."

"You think this is a regular thing for me?" she rolled her eyes at the thought.

"Criminals usually get caught in a crime cycle after all," he shot back, removing his phone from his ear and hanging up.

It wasn't long until an unmarked police car parked on the side of the road, interrupting their chat. The door opened, and out came a man sporting your stereotypical 'cop-esque' moustache.

"Joe, perfect timing," Charlie praised, uncrossing his arms.

"Jeez, what happened here?" Joe asked, releasing a low whistle for effect.

"I presume Willa, here, got jealous of the mannequin's style."

"He has the wrong person, Joe. Please tell him to let me go," she begged, hoping the new arriving officer would see reason.

"I'd prefer if you called me Officer Mark, thank you very much." Willa scrunched her face at Joe's words and looked over at Charlie, who'd made no such rule for her to follow. Charlie just let out a brisk laugh in response.

"Follow me into the car, miss. We're taking you in for questioning," Joe stated. His moustache was twitching away with every consonant.

"No," she jolted back again. While she knew they were somewhat safe people, her instincts kept her wary.

"Are you disobeying police orders?" Charlie asked, taking hold of her shoulders and physically guiding her into the car. She felt she didn't have another option at this point, so she followed without disruption.

"Where's your car, Ericson?" Joe called out as Willa climbed into the back.

"My wife dropped me in," Charlie replied, shutting the door behind her. As Charlie made his way to the passenger seat, Willa watched Joe mouth a response she couldn't hear. Charlie shook his head, dodging the comment – whatever it was, he didn't like it. Interesting, she thought. Joe climbed in shortly after and put his keys into the ignition. With a slight jingle, the car started, and they began their journey.

"I have to make a call for local security to secure the shop while we're gone, so please keep your manners and stay quiet," Charlie taunted.

an eerie vibe lurked into the room. This 'Sloppy Joe' seemed dangerous. She even wished for Rome to come and join them. Where was he? Could he see over here?

"The lady who owns that store… She's a good friend of my mother's. Did you know that?" he approached.

"No, I didn't. I don't even know who you are." Willa felt cautious.

"Look, Willa. I don't enjoy doing nothing. I know they don't give me the hard jobs around here," he admitted.

"That's unfortunate…" Willa was unsure where to go with the conversation, and his eyes showed a little more than determination.

"Yours might not be a hard case, Miss Triston, but I'm going to be the one to crack it," he leaned forward.

"I really, really think you should rethink whatever you're thinking," Willa said. Her arms itched to jolt back, but they were held in place by the handcuffs connected to the table. Noticing her urge, Joe slammed his hand down next to hers. He looked at her face through dark lashes, and his eyes filled with distrust.

Goosebumps resentfully spread onto Willa's skin as a chill rippled through the air, rolling down her spine. Joe's hands crept along the table, moving his fingers closer and closer. After a few torturous seconds, he clutched Willa's small forearms. Her breathing became sharp, and his grasp tightened… and tightened… and tightened.

"You're hurting me," she said through gritted teeth.

It was painful, primarily because it was her injured arm. In the station's light, you could already see bruising appear.

"You'll confess if it hurts," he seethed, jolting her right arm.

She yelped in pain, feeling her wrist momentarily popping out of place, and screamed for help. A wicked smirk took shape on Joe's face, but before he could make his next move, Willa began kicking her legs, jabbing Joe in the shins more than once.

"You're harming a police officer?" Joe asked crookedly, as a tear leaked from her eye. He'd breached her tough exterior.

"Just let me go!" she shouted, and to her surprise, he followed by lightening his grip. A clanging sound caught Willa's attention as Rome barged through the door, assessing the situation. Joe let her hand go in an instant, ready to lie to his boss.

"What's going on?" Rome asked, narrowing his eyes.

Willa let out a heart-wrenching sigh, and it caught his attention. Rome's eyes scanned over her; a tear was rolling down her face, her arms were shivering, and her wrists were marked in the shape of large fingers.

"What did you do?" he snapped, glaring at Joe.

"Nothing," Joe deflected.

"These marks aren't nothing!"

"I figured I'd just do a bit of roughhousing to get a confession. You know how it goes, Sheriff," Joe spoke as if it were protocol.

Rome's face twitched in rage. "Get out of this room. Now."

"Sir, I think you're overreacting..." Joe said, offended.

Rome ignored his claim and blocked Willa from Joe's view. He pulled a key from his pocket, quickly unlocking her cuffs. At that moment, Willa didn't know whether to feel relief or break into a full cry. She'd been begging all night for this result, but Joe made her feel so unsettled that she wasn't in a mood to cheer.

Joe stood in irritation. "What are you doing?"

"I'm letting her go. She clearly didn't do it!" Rome let it slip as if he knew this whole time.

"Wait. What?" Willa felt stunned. Was he really saying what she thought he said?

"How do you know for sure?" Joe challenged.

"She was just in the wrong place at the wrong time, and I wanted to see if she could help us while we still had the upper hand... then you have to go and do this?" Rome put his palm to his face.

"You detained me for your own gain? You're both sick." A vein throbbed on Willa's forehead, giving a clue to just how frustrated she felt.

Rome sighed, knowing the situation had turned into a legally liable mess. He finished taking away her handcuffs, and Willa sprung up.

"Joe, you're suspended from work without pay. I don't want to see you anywhere near this precinct for a while," Rome ordered.

"—For how long?" Joe asked, knowing fully well that he deserved it.

"Until I say so," Rome reaffirmed. He was cutting him off, and he wanted Joe to know it.

"That won't make us even," Willa threatened. After a night of torment, she'd finally gained the upper hand.

"Look, I'll do anything to settle this," Rome admitted, searching for a way to get out of trouble.

Willa nudged past him, planning to walk away from it all – out of the precinct and back into her safe, warm apartment. But when she faced Joe on equal grounds, she paused. Willa was by no means a violent person, but she needed an outlet for her anger. She was detained for so long, despite being innocent, and even got hurt in the process. If she wasn't going to be violent, she needed something else to feel at ease.

"I want him fired." She stared deep into Joe's angry eyes before turning her face to the Sheriff for his verdict.

"Willa, I can't just—" he stopped himself short.

Rather than compromising, she stood waiting for his answer to change because she knew it would. Sure, simple assault isn't always fireable in the force, and the suspension covered his bases… but as she watched his resolve unravel under her piercing stare, she guessed Rome wanted him gone just as bad as she did.

"Fine. You heard her," Rome sighed. "You know this has been a long time coming. Pack your things."

That was all Willa needed to hear, and she trailed the path to the exit.

She tried to ignore the rumble of Joe's complaints that followed, but just as she opened the door to her freedom, she heard Rome's stern voice loud and clear.

"You did this to yourself, Joe."

Chapter Three

The sun was finally up, putting an end to a night that seemed to drag on forever. Willa was standing out the front of her class with a textbook in hand, exhausting her last chance to read up on exam material. After everything, she was still determined and hoped she'd do well, but rather than worrying about herself, something else was bothering her. As her eyes darted around her, she realised her friend hadn't arrived yet.

Willa stood up straight to get a better view, craning her neck around nervously until she spotted a particular blonde, one who wore a bright green ribbon as a headband. "Poppy!" Willa called out, grabbing her attention.

"Thank gosh, I made it in time!" she exhaled, reaching the front of the class line. Once she took Willa's image in, she gasped.

"What is it?" Willa asked, concerned that there was a last-minute topic she forgot to study.

"What happened to your arm?" her eyes widened.

After waking up earlier in the morning, Willa realised her arm was more purple than she'd like it to be. So, she had to do a quick, inconvenient visit to the doctors, where they then bound her up and placed her arm in a sling.

"Oh, I tripped over," Willa said, brushing over the fact that she hurt it while running from a crime scene… and that the injury became worse from a violent police officer. Fortunately, Joe's pressure marks were out of view.

Poppy glanced at Willa in disbelief. She wasn't known to be so clumsy, but their lecturer Professor Hobbs opened the exam hall doors before she could ask for more.

"Once you go inside, you are to get started immediately. I assume you all know the general rules from previous exams, no talking, no sharing, etcetera?" Hobbs was strict, but his aged, gentle voice reassured everyone that they would do fine.

"Yes," a chorus of students responded.

"Good." He turned, ready for students to go inside until he saw someone approaching.

The hushed crowd murmured as a tall woman came into view. She had dark hair, sporting brand-named sunglasses, and an outfit to match. She oozed confidence, an emotion reinforced by being famously recognised. A gleeful look washed over Hobbs' face as he took in her presence.

"Well, I'll be damned. It seems we have quite an impressive guest to help watch over the exam this morning," he said.

"Good morning, Professor. It's a pleasure to see you again," the woman reached out an elegant hand, one Hobbs grasped in a professional shake.

He turned to address the class. "Everyone, though I'm sure you already know, this is Annabel Hale. It seems she'll be joining us today."

Poppy subtly nudged Willa's rib with her elbow, catching her attention. "Didn't she go viral last year for being a quack?"

The question baffled Willa. "Where'd you hear that?"

"It was all over the news?" Poppy answered.

"Maybe in your tabloids, but Annabel is a genius. Everything she believes is known to be spot on. She's not just a scientist; she's practically a goddess," Willa replied.

"Whatever you say. Either way, this lady won't help me pass the exam." Poppy gulped.

Willa gave her a reassuring smile and pat on the back, before focusing so hard on Annabel's face she could bore a hole in it.

"Thanks for the warm welcome," Annabel spoke, pushing her sunglasses to the top of her head. "I came by to wish you all the best of luck for this exam. I'm so proud that more and more people are showing an interest in environmental sustainability. It's because of you I have hope for our planet."

"That's so cheesy," Poppy whispered.

"Poppy, don't mess with me," Willa joked, but after two comments in a row, the warning grew severe.

"And we're delighted to have you. Well, without further delay, let's get everyone inside and begin, shall we?" Hobbs smiled, before leading the way. As the students piled inside, Willa's nerves hiked up. Act natural, she thought, as she bounced on the balls of her feet. Being the suck-up that she was, Willa even greeted Annabel on the way in.

The pair went to the back-left corner of the classroom as everyone else walked to their favourite desks. They chose this spot to give their exam papers some privacy, not because they worried about being copied, but feeling unprepared, they didn't want people to see their answers.

Willa took a seat and perused the task at hand. The paper asked her to explain how butterflies could be useful in balancing natural life, detailing the biological intricacies involved. Sure, Willa could harp on for hours about general sustainability, but she didn't really know the science behind it. Did they even have this concept in the prep questions? With her lack of study and sleep, her mind drew a blank.

All she could think about was how the two figures she saw last night looked like ants from her bedroom window. But the test wasn't asking about ants. With a shake of her head, she drew herself back to the task at hand. She had to think of something simple so that she wouldn't have a knowledge gap when explaining, but it also had to be effective. Suddenly, an idea came to her, and as the clock ticked away, she began writing paragraph after paragraph.

***

While the students appeared to be in the zone, Annabel beamed with excitement. Everyone was so interested in what they were writing, and it sparked Annabel's curiosity. She began pacing up and down the rows, zigzagging from front to back. Though she wasn't lingering, she could gather the general topics that the students addressed. Some plans seemed generic, some more appropriate than others. Whatever it was, Annabel still hadn't found a piece of work that deeply resonated with her cause. She was here on a personal mission, and that was to scout someone worthy.

Willa looked up, half startled when she saw someone was standing next to her.

Annabel Hale was reading her ten-step plan, and Willa almost bowed her head in shame. This felt half-assed. She wanted to be more prepared when showcasing her work to Annabel.

However, while Willa noticed Annabel skim past the other students, she lingered over her, reading everything Willa had written so far.

"Hmm..." Annabel sounded. Willa looked up at Annabel's face with worry, but her smile showed the 'hmm' wasn't out of disapproval. Instead, Annabel appeared genuinely intrigued. "What was your name?"

"Willa," she answered coyly.

"What an effective concept!" Annabel praised quietly and walked onwards.

Her heels clacked down the classroom's hall until she reached the front and began quietly conversing with Professor Hobbs.

While peering at the head of the classroom, Willa caught a glance at the clock and realised she had little time left. Motivated by the sudden boost from *the* Annabel Hale, she stuck her head down and continued writing – until her pencil went blunt and her plan was complete.

"Time's up, folks. Put your pens down immediately and remain seated until all test papers are collected," Hobbs stated.

The class chattered amongst themselves as they awaited collection, then exited the hall entirely. Finally, after a moment of silence, Poppy spoke up. "Alright, I officially flunked that whole thing. I won't be surprised if I have to repeat the semester."

"Poor Hobbs," Willa teased. "But don't worry, I'm in the same boat."

The pair began walking towards the university gates, where the joys of public transport awaited them. Willa let out a yawn, her lack of sleep was finally catching up with her.

"I'll see you when the results are out." Poppy tapped her on the shoulder to say goodbye before she ran toward the bus terminal.

"See you!" Willa shouted after her. She took a moment to roll her neck and shoulders around and then inspected her arm in its sling.

"Well, that's inconvenient, isn't it?" a man commented, and the voice sounded like it came right out of her mind. Willa furrowed her brows, scanning her surroundings and doubling over a certain someone that caught her attention. Sheriff Rome Pendleton was leaning against the gates.

Willa felt like her blood was boiling. "What are you doing here?"

He approached her swiftly. "I thought I'd check in to see how you're doing."

"You say that as if we're well acquainted." Willa spat back, aware of the shivers running up her arms. He wasn't someone she trusted, and she didn't enjoy the familiarity.

"Look, I'm sorry about what happened last night."

"I'd prefer if we act like it never happened," she dismissed. She'd gotten her revenge, and while that was all she needed, Rome wasn't backing down.

"That would be nice…" he drew on, "but because of you, we're understaffed at the station, and there's still an open investigation."

"You're saying that's my fault?" she spoke through gritted teeth. She didn't want to create a scene on campus where people were always on the hunt for gossip. There were already a few students gathering around, wondering why the town's Sheriff approached her.

"Well, you are directly linked, your fault or not."

"Would you mind following me for a moment?" Willa asked, grabbing his hand with her good arm instead of waiting for permission. She led them to a garden maintenance area, where two water tanks came into view and pushed Rome in between them.

"Jeez, was that necessary?" he rubbed the shoulder she pushed.

"Listen here, Rome. Joe's misconduct was not my fault, so first of all, stop the victim-blaming," she said fiercely.

"Yes, but—"

"Also, if you want to speak to me, don't show up here in your uniform, where everyone will assume things. I'm not a criminal, so don't treat me like one."

"Fine, I guess this was out of line," he admitted.

"Now, what do you want from me?" Willa crossed her arms, waiting impatiently for his reply.

"I wanted to tell you about the break-in last night. We've caught the people at fault." He ran a hand through his soft brown hair.

"Why are you telling me this?"

"I thought you'd be curious. I didn't want your midnight adventure to go to waste." He let out a sincere chuckle.

She leaned back against one of the tanks, no longer blocking his pathway – not that she could stop him if it came down to it, anyway.

She took a deep breath and organised her thoughts. She still didn't know if he was a good person, and there was obvious corruption within his workplace – Joe made that clear. But last night was just a cruel mistake on his end, and she could admit that this was a kind gesture. "Well, sure. Thanks for the heads up."

"Did you want to hear more?" he asked.

"Isn't that against the rules? Don't you have to keep cases to yourself?"

"I feel like I owe you, don't take it too personally."

She took a moment wondering what she was getting into. "Fine, enlighten me."

"Lucky for us, the store across the road ended up having security cameras. So, it seems you were telling the truth about the flashing lights."

Her mind clung to the idea of those lights. It was obvious Rome knew they would hold her attention. "Go on."

"These guys... they're electricians. They were messing around with underground wiring in front of the boutique when a wild cable went loose, whipping into the glass. The sudden impact caused it to shatter."

"The flashing light was a live cable...?"

"Indeed, it was."

"What's going to happen to the electricians? Will they get into much trouble? I mean, it was only their job, right?"

"Well, I did some calling around, and it turns out they weren't authorised to be touching those cables in the first place."

"Hmm," Willa sounded.

"They aren't revealing the purpose of what they were doing, but we've got the video footage as evidence, so we don't exactly need a confession."

"What's the punishment for tampering with government cables?"

"I'd say around six months' probation and a pretty hefty fine, depending on the judge," Rome informed.

"Interesting... Well, I better be off. I can't exactly say that it's been a pleasure seeing you, but thanks for letting me know about the situation." Willa stepped away from the tank she was leaning on and walked out into the open, letting him step out easier. "Bye, Pendleton."

"Wait up," he said, catching up to her. He walked forward and looked her over, furrowing his brows.

"What is it now?"

"Give me your number."

"Excuse me?"

"Chill out, Willa. If the investigation goes further, I might need a witness," he excused.

She pulled out her phone, passing it to him with a huff.

"Rome... Pendleton... there. Call me if you need anything," he said, punching in his number. His phone buzzed in his pocket, meaning that he sent through a text to himself to get her details.

"Fine, as long as this means you won't suddenly visit my classes," Willa warned.

Rome grinned for a moment, cutting his expression short when he saw Willa stretch out her right shoulder. His eyes looked over her sling with a mix of concern and guilt before reaching out to inspect it himself. Willa cleared her throat to draw a line, and his hand retreated.

"Bye, Rome," Willa said. She walked away, happy that the situation had come to a close. By no means was he her favourite person, but she guessed he wasn't a bad guy after all.

Willa stood at the gate, briefly scanning Platform 1 of the bus terminal to see whether Poppy was still there. Instead, she saw a cute, petite blonde with a green bow from her distance, hugging a taller, goofy-looking boy. Sure, their public display of affection disgusted most, especially Willa, but Poppy and her boyfriend both adored each other, and their happiness made Willa happy.

With that simple thought refreshing her strange morning, Willa walked to Platform 2, boarding the next bus that would take her home.

And then Willa slept for a very long time.

Chapter Four

Willa sat at a cafe on the outskirts of town, near her local clinic. It wasn't a largely populated area, so she felt comfortable enough to sit back and relax. She hunched over, sipping the straw of an iced coffee that rested on the table while flipping through a newspaper.

It had been almost a week since her exam and since she last saw Rome, which meant two things: Firstly, her exam results will be released soon. This particular detail wasn't one she welcomed wholeheartedly, but she was still curious to see how she went. Secondly, on a more exciting note, she was due for her next doctor's appointment and might be able to get rid of her sling within the hour.

As Rome had previously commented, it was entirely an inconvenience. Willa was someone who was nowhere near ambidextrous, so she had difficulty with the limited use of her right hand.

Unfortunately, Rome lingered in her mind more than she wished. That night was probably the most exciting thing she'd ever experienced, and she couldn't help but relive it. She looked down at her wrists and forearms, where the bruises were only now fading. It was painful, but the healing process was intriguing.

Willa continued to flip through the pages, arching an eyebrow as a full-page story popped out at her. It headlined 'Tradesmen Rack Up Electric Fine', with a picture of two men walking down the courthouse steps. "It's them," Willa said, leaning down to take another sip.

As she read on, she noted that the two men had been fired from their jobs not long ago, because again, they messed with government cables without permission. But, at the time, it wasn't a police matter because they weren't caught damaging a store in the process.

Despite it not being a massive case, she still felt tied to it. If they got caught and fired the first time, why would they want to do it again? What was their overall goal? As Willa sipped away, her straw began to make a suction noise, and she noticed she'd finished her drink.

She realised she had been sitting at the cafe for a while now. Turning her left hand over, she peered at her watch and saw that her appointment was in 10 minutes. She quickly stood up, placing her empty cup in the nearby recycling bin, called out thanks to the waitress, then ran out of the shop.

An unforgettable smell wafted into her nose when she opened the cafe door. At first, it was merely unfamiliar, but the more she sniffed around, she was reminded of poorly cooked meals she and Poppy used to make in a cooking class the year before. For a moment, it was the kind of smell that made her wish she bought some food with her iced coffee. But then, some other notes appeared – burned charcoal, and an odour that almost made her stomach lurch. She quickly peered around, searching for the source of the smell, but she saw nothing.

The hospital was near the cafe, and within it was the private clinic. Willa took off with a quick pace and found her way to the front entrance. However, this entrance was congested. Ambulance sirens wailed on approach to the building, giving her an eerie feeling. Something terrible must have happened, but she tried not to give it any further thought. She learned the hard way about sticking her nose in things she shouldn't.

She changed route and walked to a side door, with direct entry to the clinic. She caught the attention of the receptionist and logged her arrival.

"Dr. Whitman shouldn't be too long." He smiled, directing her to the waiting room with a gesture. She sat down and reached to grab a magazine, but by the time she decided which one she wanted, the receptionist got her attention.

"Willa, Dr. Whitman can see you now," he said.

"Right, okay," she said, stepping up out of her seat and following him to the familiar room. The receptionist opened the office door, then returned to his desk.

"Willa, how are you feeling today?" Dr. Whitman smiled. He was a younger doctor, maybe early thirties – an age where some people would question his medical competency.

"Much better, definitely ready to get rid of this ridiculous sling," she laughed, sitting down on the roller chair across from him.

"What was it you did again?" his eyes lingered on her arm. Willa knew he'd seen Joe's marks on her wrist when she first came by, but she wasn't prepared to dive into the story with him.

"It was a nasty fall." She stuck to her half-truth.

He paused, making eye contact. His expression revealed his hesitation. "Right, I remember now. Can you move it around for me?"

Willa followed his direction, gently twisting her wrist and extending her elbow. She looked up again, waiting for his assessment.

"Well, it all seems to be healing the way it should. You're going to be happy; let's get that sling off." He smiled.

"Thank goodness," she sighed in relief, quickly untying the material knot on her left shoulder and gently releasing her arm.

"The bruises should go away in the next few days, so avoid bumping into anything on that side. It could be a bit tender," he informed.

"Of course."

"Otherwise, you're free to go."

Willa stood up from her seat and offered a warm smile. "Thank you very much."

"One more thing," he stopped her. "Try to avoid any nasty falls in the future. Maybe stay away from certain staircases that could cause them, okay?"

She knew what he was referring to; by saying 'certain staircases' he meant 'certain people'. However, she didn't expect to see Joe ever again.

"Thanks for your concern, but you don't need to worry." Her eyes showed a glint of promise, and he nodded in response.

Willa turned to the door, ready to walk back through the hallway. However, a sudden thought came to mind, and she turned around once more.

"I'm just wondering, did you happen to know what's going on outside?" his joyous expression dampened as if Willa poured chilling water over him, snapping him back to reality.

"Well, there isn't much we can say, other than it's quite an unfortunate sight."

"Ah... that it is." Willa turned back around and made her way towards the front desk.

Doctor appointments were expensive, especially as a university student. Even with a certain extent of health insurance, Willa was nervous about picking up the bill. As Willa waited for the friendly, greying receptionist to ring up her price, she reached into her handbag for her wallet, ready to pay her fees.

"It looks like you're fine to go."

"Isn't the general cost $50?" she shook her head.

His face pinched, echoing the same confusion she felt. "Weren't you aware? While you were inside, your relative paid the fee."

"My relative? That must be a mistake. Did you catch their name?"

"Hmm, Venice?"

She let out an annoyed groan. "You've got to be kidding me."

"No, wait, it's written here...right, his name is—"

"Thanks," she interrupted, walking away from the desk.

Once the hospital doors shut behind her, she grasped her phone and searched for the source of her anger. Rome Pendleton.

Willa didn't hear the ring of the dial tone for long. She'd soon find out Rome had a habit of answering phones too promptly – to almost a competitive degree.

"Good afternoon, Willa," he answered with a deep voice.

"Are you stalking me or something?" Willa got straight to the point.

"I mean, I wouldn't call it stalking." His voice sounded surprised.

"How did you know when my appointment was?"

"Uh... I did a bit of investigating?" by this point, Rome knew his efforts were in vain.

Willa looked around meekly, checking if anyone was nearby. There wasn't, and so she yelled into her phone. "Do you know how inappropriate that is?"

"Calm down, Willa. I did you a favour, didn't I?"

"An invasion of privacy isn't a favour!"

"I guess you have a point."

Willa ran to a seat nearby, too frustrated and too tired to continue standing. "You do realise that if you weren't the Sheriff, I would probably report you to the police after this?"

"I get it. It won't happen again." He paused, thinking of how to change the subject. "Hey, what are you doing now, anyway?"

"I'm sitting down, angry, on the phone to you. But wait, you can't see me, can you?" her eyes widened at the thought as she jerked around, looking over her shoulder like a crazy person.

"Jesus, no, I can't. I'm at the precinct, I was just curious," he quickly answered.

"How do I know you're telling the truth?"

"Seriously? I'll get my deputy. Hey, Charlie, can you come here for a second?" his voice became softer as he was further away from the phone.

"What is it?" Charlie asked. Willa could hear his familiar voice clearly, so it seemed he was on speaker.

"I'm just confirming that I'm at the station," he answered. While Willa's tense shoulders eased, she still felt annoyed.

"Oh. Willa... I might owe you an apology," Charlie said, referring to their last encounter. After all, he was the one that got Willa into the whole mess of things.

"I'll accept the apology if you get Rome off my back," Willa spat.

Charlie and Rome both cleared their throats awkwardly, and the phone became muffled. She could briefly hear Rome telling Charlie to go away, and it sounded like he had his hand covering the phone speaker so that she couldn't hear.

"Well, uh, moving on," Rome said.

"So, why did you do it?" Willa remembered back to last week where she was the one being asked 'why did you do it'. Somehow, she found humour in the situation.

"That's not important now, is it?"

"Actually, it is," she pressed.

"Look, even after telling you about the case, I owed you one. If you're still at the hospital, do you need a lift home? It's a bit late."

"You're my biggest threat right now, so don't taunt me with your assistance," she warned.

"Don't endanger yourself out of spite, Willa."

"Bye." She ended the call abruptly.

Honestly, a lift home could have been helpful. She didn't bring her car out today because she needed to refuel it, and that was her least favourite thing to do. Ignoring the cost factor, the smell of petrol always stuck to her, and if she wasn't able to go home and shower immediately, she preferred to take public transport.

Willa made her way to the hospital's bus stop. After sitting there for a while, she realised nothing was coming her way. She looked through the bus schedule on the poster beside her seat and muttered to herself. "Please tell me they haven't stopped… frick."

Her luck was against her, and the bus was no longer an option. She checked her phone service, then recalled there was no internet connection. The outskirts of town allowed service for phone calls, but that was it.

Usually, this wouldn't be an issue when going to call a taxi. However, Willa had never called a taxi before, and she needed the internet to search for their number.

She began to weigh her options. Walking home would take thirty minutes at the least, but calling Rome again and taking his offer would only take around ten. Plus, she'd be somewhat safe. But, despite the convenience, her pride stopped her. "I guess I'm walking."

Willa stepped away from the bus stop and began walking toward town. She was fortunate because, for most of the way, the area was well lit. She even felt safe enough to take out her earphones from her bag and plug them in.

Her playlist made the time fly by, and for the first time in her life, she volunteered to do math. Overall, it would take around thirty minutes to get home. If each song averaged out to be three minutes long, she'd only need to listen to ten songs until she saw her apartment complex. Easy, she thought.

As she walked, she set up a queue of her favourite ten songs and put her phone back in her pocket. "Nine songs left," she told herself.

Step by step, further and further, houses surrounded her. Each home held a different shape, none making any effort to fit in with the other. It was a great example of the city she lived in. Everyone existing on their own; no one worked together to improve. "Eight songs left."

Now, she headed towards the quiet part of town – an industrial estate with poor street lighting. Her instincts told her to run through it, but she tried to ignore them. Looking down, she had neither the right shoe choice, nor the stamina. "Seven songs left."

Here, she was walking through what she thought would've been the worst part, but something was different. She noticed that the usually quiet and dark barren area was as bright as the rest of the stretch.

"Hmm." There were no looming streetlamps, so she wondered where the light was coming from. This seventh song felt like it went slower and slower, and she didn't know whether it was because it was a boring choice or because she was distracted, and her nerves were getting the better of her.

But as her anxiety grew, so did her curiosity – despite where it led her last time. Finally, she began to recognise something familiar. The light started to flicker. It was a short moment, and the bright white light illuminated the area around.

"Power surges…" she spoke to herself, realising there was the same flashing effect as the week before. It was as if her body became possessed by the allure of the light and she was drawn in, closer and closer. Then, walking beyond a pile of old cars, Willa found a spot where she could both see what was going on and hide at the same time.

Once again, two men were standing around an underground cable system, and from this close distance, she could properly make out their faces. They were the same faces from the news story, the one she had read earlier that evening. So, why were they still messing with underground cables?

She took out her phone, ensuring that the flash was turned off, and snapped a quick picture of their illuminated faces. Willa leaned down, further concealing herself behind the old car, and quickly pressed 'Rome Pendleton' in her recent calls. Once again, he immediately picked up the phone. "Look, I'm sorry—" he began, but Willa interrupted.

"I'm sending you a picture now, I'm on Marksman Avenue, and I've found the electricians again."

"Wait. What? Willa, get away from there!"

She worried that his voice was too loud, even without being on speaker. "Shh, keep your voice down," she whispered. "I might be able to find out what they're doing if I stay here a bit longer."

"Don't—" he began once more, only for Willa to cut him off again.

"Don't call me back. They might hear the vibration. You know where I am," she whispered, hanging up the call after.

Willa quickly set up the voice recorder on her phone. If she heard anything, she was going to make sure she had proper evidence of it. She sat silently and listened to the echoing of tools, and as the lights continued to flicker, she waited for any conversation they might come up with. Anything that could give out a clue as to what they were doing.

"At least there aren't any shops around to accidentally damage," the younger man's voice said as the flickering continued.

The older voice gruffly replied with, "You need to shut up and stop losing control of the cables."

"I know, I know."

"If we continue to do a sloppy job, we're gonna have to pay everything back. You understand?" the older man warned.

"You don't think they'll make us do that, do you?" the younger man sounded worried. "I've already spent half of my advance!"

"Then you better stop getting us in trouble! Plus, who cares about the advance. I've got my eye on the million at the end!"

A million dollars? Her mouth dropped. So they were paid to do this – whatever they were doing. Not just a simple sum, but one million dollars! Willa sat back, ready to listen for more.

"Who has that kind of money, anyway?" the younger man spoke in awe.

"We're not supposed to know. Just do your job, find the money

magically in your bank, and be done with it," the older man grumbled.
They didn't know. It was an anonymous contractor.

Interrupting her thoughts, Willa heard the wail of police sirens and a car stopped right nearby the older car she was resting on.

Rome had arrived.

Chapter Five

Shortly after Rome exited his vehicle, another police car arrived. It was Charlie.

Willa peeped out from behind the car, noticing the two electricians were trying to scurry away. Before they could gain any ground, Rome's long strides reached them.

"Police! Stop where you are!" he called out with assertion, pulling his gun from his side holster, and the two men froze in place.

"Shit, what happened now?" the older man shouted, slapping his younger accomplice across the back of the head in blame.

"I didn't do anything!" the younger man defended.

"Charlie, come and sort these two out," Rome said, throwing Charlie another pair of cuffs.

"Righto, boss," Charlie caught them and turned toward the duo. "Get on the ground!"

The men complied without hesitation – their resolve to escape diminishing after being held at gunpoint. Charlie walked over to them, cuffing each one's hands behind their backs.

"Well, if it isn't Ron and Dave Donohugh. I thought you'd have learned your lesson by now about tampering with things you shouldn't," Rome stated, clearly addressing the two criminals by their names.

Ron and Dave Donohugh, Willa made a mental note for future research. With the same surnames, it seems they were related, just as she wondered last week.

"Get up and walk to the car," Charlie commanded.

Willa, still hidden, watched the two men struggle to get up off the ground, squirming around until they finally got to their feet. Rome kept his gun pointed at Ron and Dave until Charlie had safely locked them in the car.

"Get them to the station. I'll follow you shortly," Rome told Charlie.

"Yes sir."

Charlie jumped into the driver's side of his car, started the engine, and then sped away towards town.

Rome put his gun in his holster and looked around hurriedly. "Willa? You can come out!"

Willa stood out from behind the car, and Rome relaxed his tense shoulders. She threw her phone at him, hoping that he'd catch it, and thankfully he did.

"Press play. You can thank me later," Willa said, walking to his police car.

"Hold up a second – what on Earth were you thinking?" Rome scolded, cornering her against the car.

"Just listen—"

"No, you promise me something first, okay?" he crossed his arms. His face filled with frustration, but not wholly aimed at Willa. "I don't want you near any of these situations without me around."

"Fine, I'll be more cautious," she somewhat agreed. "But I called you right as I saw them, and you won't believe what I found."

Rome sighed, opening the passenger door. "Get in."

Willa followed his gesture and sat down while Rome reached over and buckled her in. The action was as if he was treating her like a kid, despite both being in their twenties. She tried to ignore the patronising action. After all, she didn't want to start another argument. She was desperate to talk about the footage on her phone before anything else.

He walked around to the driver's side and entered the car.

"Alright, press play when you're ready." Willa nodded at the phone still in his hands.

He opened it and sat back, but then turned over to Willa. "Are you warm enough?"

"Yes, now just listen to it!" she rolled her eyes, feeling impatience bubble up inside of her.

"Because it was quite cold out there—"

"Give it here," she said, taking her phone back into her hands and pressing play herself.

As they listened to the conversation between Ron and Dave, a grin took over Willa's face.

"A million dollars!" Rome stated, shocked.

"They were paid to do it. They're not doing it on their own," Willa confirmed.

"I can't blame them... I'd do anything for a million dollars," Rome admitted.

"I don't think you're supposed to say that as the Sheriff of our town," she said.

He chuckled and thought back over Ron and Dave's conversation. "They don't know who their benefactor is... I think this is a bigger case than we expected."

"Gee, thanks, Willa. I wouldn't have been able to figure this out without you," she teased, waiting for his appreciation.

"Thank you, honestly."

Willa sat back, the sense of accomplishment reddening her ears and blushing her cheeks.

"—But you can't keep doing this," Rome continued, turning on the car's ignition and rolling onto the road.

Her voice lowered with irritation. "What do you mean?"

"Well, if you get caught showing up around too many crime scenes, you could get into trouble."

"Then why did you involve me in the first place?" she huffed, crossing her arms and leaning further back into her seat.

"Well, I didn't know there was an entire plot at hand!" he defended, holding his hands up in a dramatic, 'I'm innocent,' act.

The car swerved in response, and Willa quickly grabbed onto the wheel. "Keep your hands on the wheel!"

"Look, I'm not saying you can't get involved. It's just that this situation can't repeat itself."

"You're confusing me."

"We need to make it a bit more official, that's all."

Willa continued to look at him with a puzzled expression.

"I'm offering for you to work by my side, only within regular hours where I can monitor you safely. You've proved yourself more useful than Charlie on this job, and with Joe gone, we're understaffed," he said.

"I'm not looking for a job, Rome."

"It's just for whenever you feel like investigating the case. Now that it's more of an organised crime situation, I'd rather you be safe and following protocols than simply doing things on your own."

"So, it's a way to keep tabs on me? That sounds wonderful," she spoke with sarcasm.

He rolled his eyes. "It's for your safety, Willa."

"Hmm."

"Do you want to be in on this investigation or not?"

"Fine, fine. Yes, I'll take your offer," Willa agreed, and Rome smirked in response.

"Great," he replied. Their talking must have taken up more time than she thought because suddenly Rome brought the car to a stop. They had arrived outside of her apartment building. Rome jumped out of his seat, skipping to the passenger door and opening it. Willa stepped out of the car and walked to the apartment complex entrance, before spinning back around.

"Wait... how did you know where I lived?"

He laughed. "Goodnight, Willa,"

***

On a fine Wednesday morning, Willa waited alongside Poppy, who wore her trademark ribbon as usual. Today, it was lilac.

"Please—" Poppy whined, desperately holding both of Willa's hands in her own.

"Poppy, I don't think I'd have the time," Willa tried to refuse awkwardly. The light from Poppy's eyes dimmed a little, but she still had hope.

"But I love this band, and I just know that you will too!" she was determined.

"You're already going with James. I don't want to be a third wheel," Willa said.

"See, you do have the time!" Poppy said, pointing her finger at Willa as if she had caught her out.

"I'm not going, okay!" Willa rolled her eyes, waiting for the topic to drop.

The girls were currently debating whether they'd be going to a concert within the upcoming month. The band was called 'The Bakery', and although it was both a timid and irrelevant name, they had some good songs. Willa liked how the band members weren't conventionally attractive, but their personalities were so cool that it made any girl fall head over heels.

Honestly, Willa would love to go to the concert. She had even looked up the dates and ensured that she had nothing planned on the days they were playing. While she admired Poppy and her boyfriend James' relationship, she didn't enjoy being ignored when they became lost in each other's eyes. A sour look took over Willa's face just thinking about it.

"... Alright?" Poppy asked.

"Huh?" Willa wondered, not paying attention to what she had said.

"Were you seriously not listening?"

"No, no, I was." A lie. A bad one.

Poppy rolled her eyes. "I was just saying when we get our results back in this next class... if I pass, will you come with me?"

Now, Willa knew Poppy wasn't the most outstanding student. She had a wonderfully bright personality, but she just didn't apply herself when it came to studying or reading her textbooks. If she agreed to Poppy's proposition, because she failed the entire last semester, there's a big chance that she won't pass this exam. It'll be an empty gesture.

"Fine, it's a deal," Willa said, shaking Poppy's hand. This way, she'll at least seem supportive.

"Thank you, thank you!" she practically squealed, shaking Willa's hands up and down.

Willa laughed at her friend's antics. "Alright, we better head inside and get a good seat."

Once again, Willa and Poppy walked up to their favourite spot; the back left corner. Willa lazily plunked herself down while Poppy practically floated in her seat. Of course, their movements contrasted each other, but they enjoyed each other's differences the most.

The room went quiet as Professor Hobbs arrived, ready for the lesson to begin. However, the class started whispering again when another person followed his entrance.

Just like last week, Annabel Hale was here. At this rate, Willa worried that she'd get used to seeing her around.

As hard as it was, Willa told herself not to get too attached. She sighed, feeling a little creepy.

"Welcome back, students," Hobbs began, "I'd just like to applaud you all for your efforts in last week's exam."

Willa reached down into her bag and grabbed out her water bottle. Then, looking to her side, she noticed Poppy had already opened up the website that sold concert tickets on her phone. She was eager, that's for sure.

Annabel positioned herself against the whiteboard at the front, taking in the room.

"Now, I'm going to go around with our tutors and hand out the results. I know you've all been anxiously waiting for them," he grinned, dividing his pile of exam results into three.

"Make sure not to spread your results around, alright?" Hobbs said, addressing the general academic rules that no one followed.

"Promise to tell me how you go, okay?" Poppy whispered, peering away from her phone for a split second.

"Of course," Willa responded with a quiet laugh.

Willa sat back, sipping from her water bottle. Her phone buzzed in her pocket, and she unlocked it, seeing who it was from. Rome.

R: How'd you go?

She tapped away at her phone's keyboard, watching people's results get delivered in the corner of her eye.

W: How'd I go with what?

R: You get your exam results back today, don't you?

Willa laughed a humourless laugh and looked back down to her phone.

W: You shouldn't know that. Anything new with the case?

R: Not yet. Because Ron and Dave don't even know who their benefactor is, interrogating them didn't get us far.

W: Well then, don't message me.

Her reply may have been blunt, but she wasn't in a place where she wanted to have 'small talk' with her new 'coworker.'

R: Sheesh.

His reply was all she needed to put her phone back into her pocket. As she took another large mouthful of water, she noticed Professor Hobbs was walking towards her and Poppy. He passed over Poppy's results first, and his face remained friendly, yet stoic. However, once he handed Willa her works, his face grew into a wrinkled smile. Willa tried to swallow her water as she took the paper from his hands. But it didn't manage to go down. This left Willa with similar-looking cheeks to a chipmunk.

"Congratulations, Willa. High Distinction. Keep it up," he quietly commended.

Willa's eyes grew, and she coughed out, startled by the result. Water spluttered through her lips, and she quickly covered her mouth with her spare hand.

Professor Hobbs handed out the other papers, acting as if her embarrassing dribbling never occurred, but Willa couldn't believe what he'd just said.

"What? You got a HD?" Poppy's voice was higher than usual. "I thought you said you blundered that exam?"

"I thought I did too," Willa admitted, wiping the water from her arm onto her shirt. Even if Annabel told her she had an effective concept, it didn't mean she met the criteria. The rest of her paper had the potential to be garbage. "How did you go?"

"Well, I don't want to say after your result," Poppy joked sheepishly. Poppy looked down at her result properly, and Willa was hoping she'd be free from having to go to the concert.

"Don't be silly," she coaxed.

"I passed, Willa!" she said, eagerly grabbing her phone out to purchase the tickets.

"Great job!" Willa replied with a smile, half genuine, half drained, knowing that answer sealed her third-wheeling fate.

As Willa looked around the room, still feeling a bit chuffed about her result, she noticed that Professor Hobbs and his teaching staff had all finished handing out their piles. They were now walking back to the front.

Finally, Annabel stepped forward. Her designer heels clacking pleasantly with each step she took, sounding almost like music to Willa's ears. *Such a creep.*

"Well, now that everyone has their results, I believe you all did well," Annabel began, looking around with pride. "I read over each of the exams that you submitted, and I was pleased to see all the hard work people put into their ten-step plans."

Willa smiled, pretending Annabel spoke to her specifically. But as she watched on, she began to realise Annabel was staring in her direction.

"I've come back today because there was a particular submission that sparked my interest. Not only was it an example of thinking out of the box, but it was also wonderfully detailed."

"Now, I'm going to read out the student number of this particular student, and if it is you, please check your emails shortly. I will officially invite the successful student to a formal dinner, filled with my professional friends and associates," Annabel explained.

Whispers broke out throughout the class' auditorium, and Willa knew the exact reason why. Nowadays, industry connections were everything. It didn't matter how many clubs you participated in as a student or how great an intern you might've been at a specific company. An invitation to this formal dinner is practically a golden, one-way ticket to a successful career.

Even Poppy knew how important this opportunity was, despite her lack of interest in the subject. She was already leaning forward in her chair, waiting to hear those golden digits.

Willa quickly reached into her pocket and grabbed out her phone, taking off its case. Here was where she kept a few essential cards, as she found it was easier than rummaging through an old wallet.

She grasped at her ID card, trying to avoid looking at the awful ID photo as per usual, and looked at the student number written on it.

"The student number of this particular person is…" she paused for effect.

"E234…"

Willa read along on her card as Annabel spoke… E234.

"–67."

"67."

"–85."

"–85."

"Holy shit," she whispered, drawing Poppy's attention.

Willa's eyes widened, and she almost choked for the second time. However, this time she wasn't even drinking water.

The praised submission was her own. She'd won the golden ticket to Annabel's dinner party.

"Thank you all for your time, and thank you for being interested in saving our environment," Annabel sincerely spoke. Then, without another word, her heels click-clacked as she walked out the door.

"Was it you?" Poppy whispered excitedly, poking Willa repeatedly in the arm.

"Yeah, I think it was."

Chapter Six

It was officially the afternoon, and the precinct was dead quiet. Rome was the only person working at the time, and now that the initial questioning was over, Ron and Dave were sent out of town to a more permanent holding cell.

As they were caught in the act tampering with government circuits on two separate occasions, as well as breaching their parole, the local judge didn't hesitate to sentence them to a year of jail time.

Although this was great for the case, Rome wasn't satisfied. He had spent the entire day rocking lazily back and forth on his office chair, waiting for a potential message from Willa. Because of her silence, he concluded that his last text was far too brief and wasn't enough for her to construct a proper reply. In all honesty, he didn't even know what he'd reply to the word 'sheesh.'

He just couldn't accept the fact that his presence, either in person or on the phone, wasn't wanted. So instead, he thought about other reasons. Maybe Willa's professor confiscated her phone, or her phone died. Suddenly, his thoughts became darker. Maybe her bus crashed, and she got rushed to the hospital.

As his mind wandered, his throat grew dry, and the feeling of discomfort danced across his skin. He'd seen and heard so many tragic things through his job, and an issue with Willa would feel a bit close to home.

He cleared his throat and stretched out his neck, looking down at his computer. He wasn't an easily motivated person, but it was a simple fact that if he progressed further in the case, Willa would need to get involved again. That was currently the only thing on his mind.

Before his mind got too twisted, his phone vibrated. He breathed, feeling the initial anxiousness that anyone gets when they have a new number calling their phone, and then he pressed the little green button. "Sheriff Rome Pendleton speaking."

"Hey, Sheriff, it's Arthur Higgins," a scratchy voice greeted. "I own the 'Higgins' Electrics' company that the Donohugh boys work at."

"Oh? Go on," Rome's eyebrow arched.

"Well, there's been a bit of a situation, I guess. It usually wouldn't be that big of a deal, but seeing the Donohugh's had some kind of plan, I think you should come and take a look," Arthur said.

"Well, thanks for telling me. I'll try to be there within the next few hours," Rome said, happy with any new lead.

"Great, see you then," Arthur politely ended the call.

A smirk broke out on Rome's face as he went to his favourites page in his contacts, pressing Willa's number. Since it was just her and Charlie on the list, he didn't seem to have many other friends in town.

"What do you want?" Willa deadpanned.

"Believe it or not, Willa, we have a lead."

"Wait — really?" her voice filled with disbelief.

"I got a call from the boss of Ron and Dave, the electricians, and he's found something he thinks is suspicious. He thinks I should check it out."

A pause. "Just you?" Willa squeaked, waiting for the invitation.

"I guess it's important that you come along."

"Alright, where shall I meet you?"

"Higgins' Electrics, but I can come and get you?"

"I'll meet you there. See you in twenty minutes," she asserted, hanging up the phone abruptly.

Rome stood awkwardly, checking the clock across the room. Not wanting to waste any time, he placed his phone back in his pocket and got moving. He picked the keys up from his desk, grabbed his badge and wallet, then sprinted to the police car.

It was probably a 20-minute drive from the station, and it was likely that Willa knew that. He had no excuse to be late. Rome jumped into the front seat, cranked down the hand brake, and wheeled away from the station in a split second.

He tried not to speed but knew he couldn't control his eagerness, even if he represented the law.

***

Willa was waiting at a sign by the gates that read 'Higgins' Electrics' in fancy gold lettering. She crossed her arms in an aim to look hurried, but she didn't have anywhere else to be. And after winning dinner with her idol, she couldn't possibly feel bitter.

Willa was also excited to follow the lead. Rather than feeling like a chore, the investigation seemed like a hobby. She looked down at her watch and saw another minute pass by. "Any second now…"

As if right on cue, a police car pulled up in a hurry, raising dust behind it. The car's loud arrival startled Willa, but she quickly regained her coolish, deliberate pose.

The car door swung open carelessly, and Rome stepped out. He wore smart clothing – a white buttoned shirt rolled up to his elbows and some seven-eighth navy pin-striped pants with boat shoes. The only signifying factor that showed he worked for the police was his car and the small Sheriff badge attached to his waist.

"Was I on time?" he asked coolly.

"Only about ten seconds late, but I guess that can be forgiven," Willa joked.

The light mood surprised Rome, and his face broke out into a grin. "How'd you get here?"

"I drove since I got home early today," she said, pointing over to a modern but paint-thinning car down by a set of parks. "You ready?"

After a single nod from Rome, he pushed at the creaking, rusty gates, and she followed along.

The short, dusty driveway came to a fork – one road leading to an electric tool shed and one to a well-structured office. A few cars were parked outside with the 'Higgins' Electrics' branding painted on them.

It was your usual 'tradesman' scene, with nothing too peculiar so far. But this normalcy couldn't disguise the somewhat urgent conversation they were about to have with the business owner.

Rome continued in front, and as he reached the office door, he politely knocked. However, it wasn't your regular knock. Somehow, Rome did the most annoying knock sequence, maybe ever. The kind that made Willa think just how 'typically Rome' it was.

She scrunched her face with judgment, and when Rome noticed, he shrugged his shoulders in response.

This man was bulletproof.

The door slowly opened inwards, and a gruff, tan-looking, middle-aged man appeared.

"Sheriff, thanks for coming," he greeted kindly.

"No worries, Arthur," Rome smiled back and then pointed at Willa. "This is Willa, my colleague."

"Nice to meet you, Willa," Arthur said, holding his hand out for a handshake. She returned the pleasantries before anticipation filled the silence.

"So, what do you have for us?" Rome asked, waiting for the news.

Arthur waved them inside. "Come in. I'll show you something."

The lack of information excited Willa. Somehow, with everything still left in the dark, it made her hungrier to find out what it was.

The duo followed Arthur as he led them to a small conference room. A large desk and a bunch of chairs made up the space. On the table, Willa and Rome both noticed a big blueprint map spread out for them.

"Well, take a seat," he said to them. Rome pulled out a seat for Willa, which she graciously took, and he sat beside her.

"So, our circuits are being tampered with," he started.

"We already know about the work that Ron and Dave did," Rome added, waiting for something new.

"Well, here's the thing. It's occurred since you caught them."

Willa's eyes lit up, and her posture leaned forward, pressing him to go on.

"We'd usually disregard these things as an accidental switch-change that could happen from natural causes... you know, animals burrowing underground, strong winds on power poles, that type of thing," he began explaining.

"Right," Willa said, filling the space.

"However, after seeing Ron and Dave's tampering, it seems more deliberate."

"We thought a few people were working on getting the same result... do you know what they're doing?" Willa asked, seizing the lead.

"No, not yet... but I don't think they're anywhere near their goal," he said. Arthur's posture matched Willa's as he leaned forward, and he pointed at the blueprints. "If you look at the map, I've marked all the large underground power circuits we have around our town."

"So, the black circles..." Rome prompted, looking at the map.

"Yeah, the black circles, there's thirty-six in total," Arthur confirmed.

"What are the red circles?" Willa asked.

"Those are the circuits that look like someone has tampered with them. As you can see, there are only six red circles so far. Two were from when Ron and Dave were still working with us, two after I fired them, and two more since their arrest."

Willa looked over the red circles on the map and saw one at the outdoor shopping complex near her apartment. The night she was suspected as a thief. Willa looked at her situation now, being heavily relied on by the town's Sheriff, and laughed aloud.

"Two more in a week… they're working pretty quickly," Rome observed, scratching some stubble around his chiselled jawline.

"I thought so, too. But the funny thing is, the circuits have some protective layer added to them after they'd been tampered with. My boys were only just able to fix the circuits from the shopping complex this morning," informed Arthur.

"Really?" the point sparked Rome's interest.

"Yeah, really. If they take over too many circuits too quickly, we won't regain them fast enough. I don't know what they're planning, but these delays will have us running pretty far behind."

"So, that means we have to guard the circuit boards. If we can't fall behind, we need to think ahead," Rome concluded.

"I've got ten staff members that will be happy with some overtime," Arthur agreed.

"We only have two at the moment…" Rome uttered, disappointed.

"You mean three, right?" Willa noticed he was leaving her out.

"No, I'm not including you on this one," Rome said bluntly.

"Why not?" she asked, trying not to sound whiney.

"They strike at night, and I'm not going to leave you alone guarding a circuit board against potentially dangerous people." He left no room for discussion. "Anyway, even if we had you, we're still way understaffed."

Arthur cleared his throat. "Did you see what pace they were working at when they switched up the circuits?"

"They weren't too fast in the process… probably thirty minutes each?" Willa answered unsurely, thinking about how long she saw them through her window that first night, and then how long until she arrived at the scene.

"In that case, you don't have to worry about the big thirty-six number; twelve of us will be able to guard it easily. It's only three circuits for each of us. The circuits are barely a five-minute walk from each other," Arthur informed.

"Even if we catch them in the act, what about the protection layer?" Rome asked.

"It seems it goes on at the last minute; otherwise, they wouldn't be able to touch it to finish their work," Arthur said.

"If we rotate around every ten minutes, we'd be able to stop them," Rome concluded with a grin.

"Exactly!" Arthur exclaimed.

"Wait... Staying up all night and patrolling around every ten minutes, is that practical?" Willa spoke the harsh truth. "You all have day jobs."

"I guess, especially until we can get more people to help," Rome admitted.

"Well, what are you suggesting we do?" Arthur asked.

Willa wracked her brain for a minute or so, and the room remained quiet while Arthur and Rome also thought to themselves. Despite all of this, she couldn't help but be excited for dinner with her favourite environmentalist.

Suddenly, an idea map came into her mind.

Dinner with Annabel → dinner with environmentalists → environmentalists → saving the world → saving energy → energy → circuit boards → an idea that just might work.

"I've got it! They need electricity to switch these circuits around properly, right?"

"Well... yes," Arthur answered.

She grinned. "Then let's begin an energy-saving campaign."

"Willa..." Rome's forehead creased with doubt.

"No, seriously. If we're so understaffed, and the tampering only happens at night, it's a great idea," she said.

Arthur scratched his head in confusion. "What do you mean?"

"Just think, tell everyone in town that we're shutting off power from after midnight, like a curfew. It's a reasonable request to conserve energy. Plus, it means it cuts the patrolling down to only around four hours," Willa explained.

"What about hospitals? Or traffic lights?" Rome prompted.

"It's easy enough to set up a few generators. It won't go through to the underground circuits that they're trying to get at," Arthur piped in. "That is, if we think the situation is pressing enough to warrant it."

It was a tough call for Rome to make, but his instincts told him it had to happen. No one gets offered a million dollars to muck around. Instead, there's a much bigger, potentially dangerous plan afoot; he was sure of it.

"Yeah, I think it could be. But Arthur, you're sure the plan is possible?" Rome asked.

"Look, we might get some backlash, but it's possible. It'll probably take a week to sort."

"That's not too bad. Two more circuits changed won't be that much of a worry. Good job, Willa," Rome smiled, leaning over to pat her on the back.

Willa grinned, looking down at her hands, trying not to fidget under the attention. While she enjoyed the credit, she couldn't help but think this emotion was different to when Annabel complimented her work. Willa had a strange connection with Rome, and she almost wanted him to praise her more.

She shook her head to change her train of thought and absorbed how this plan would benefit her. She somehow shot two birds with one stone, using an idea that would help her role as an investigator and as an environmentalist. Despite everything, she almost felt proud.

Apart from some finer details to be confirmed, their plan was sorted, so they wrapped things up with Arthur and said their goodbyes. Willa and Rome walked out the door and made their way down the short, dusty driveway.

"So, how did your test go?" Rome asked for the second time that day.

She smiled. "Honestly… I did really well."

He laughed in response. "No wonder you're in such a good, non-argumentative mood."

"Hey!"

"In all seriousness, I'm relieved. I'd feel a little guilty if you failed," Rome said, referring to keeping her away from studying late into the night with Joe.

"Well, if I didn't pass, I would blame you," she said bluntly.

He laughed. "I'd expect nothing less."

They reached the gates and Willa stopped, turning to look directly at him with a coy smirk. "Actually, I didn't just pass. I got the best in the cohort."

"What? That's great!" Rome said, breaking into a sincere grin. His hand went up for a high five, and Willa happily followed through with the gesture.

"Also… It means I won a chance to have dinner with an esteemed environmentalist," she continued grinning.

"A dinner date? With whom?" he asked, turning slightly rigid.

"Annabel Hale and a bunch of her house guests in the same profession," she said.

"Annabel Hale?" he thought for a moment before deciding he approved. "That's pretty cool, Willa."

She pulled out her keys. "Anyway, I better go. Catch you later, partner."

"You too, partner," Rome chuckled, watching her get into her car and speed away. "It's only Annabel Hale. What a relief."

Chapter Seven

Surrounded by a hum of chatter and a strong smell of coffee beans, Willa felt content with how she'd decided to spend her Friday afternoon.

She was currently sitting at a local cafe called 'Christmas in a Cup'. Sure, the place's name was a bit cheesy, but it sold some good hot chocolates, and it helped that Poppy worked here.

"Are you sure you won't get in trouble because I'm putting these posters up?" Willa asked, whipping her head back around to face Poppy.

"I'm the life of this place. They'd never get mad at me, plus they're already too worried that I'll leave," Poppy laughed from behind the counter.

Willa looked back at the giant corkboard used for local advertisements and finished pinning a poster. As she stood back, she noticed her A3 size poster attracted more attention than the other adverts.

"I can't believe you're actually cutting the town's power," Poppy said in awe.

The poster was an official announcement that Willa designed, and she even got a seal of approval from the environmental firm that Annabel Hale worked at.

Though they kept the cause of the power cuts a secret, they had to alert the public about the power shutting off in general. Despite the possibility of some backlash from local night owls or late-night gamers, this project seriously boosted Willa's name within environmentalist circles.

Willa grinned. "Do you think Professor Hobbs would be proud? Maybe I'm his next Annabel Hale."

"Unfortunately, I think you'd still have to travel quite a distance to get that far up his ass," Poppy replied with a laugh.

"Poppy, think of the customers!" Willa scrunched her nose with a chuckle. But even she knew the few older customers dining in weren't bothered by her metaphor.

"So how did you get electrical companies to agree? Wouldn't it be a major profit loss?"

Willa paused, trying to think of a plausible excuse that wouldn't bring up the actual case.

"I went and pitched the idea to the Sheriff, and it seemed like he's quite an environmentalist... So, I guess he was very onboard with using his authority to make it happen," she fibbed.

"You went to the Sheriff?" Poppy's mouth dropped.

"Yes?"

"What was he like?" Poppy ran over from behind the counter, dragging Willa to a free table.

"Rome's actually kind of annoying," Willa said without a second thought.

"Rome?" Poppy repeated in the form of a question. A knowing smirk came onto her face, and Willa groaned.

"That's his name. Am I not supposed to use it?" Willa retorted.

"No, no, you can. It just makes you sound quite familiar with him." Poppy grinned, her head now resting on one of her hands as her eyes became large saucers.

"Leave it, Poppy," Willa warned.

"Well, why is he annoying?"

"Self-absorbed, sarcastic, spam texts, basically the general definition of annoying behaviour."

"You text each other?" Poppy shouted.

"Shh – yes, just about the project arrangements, I swear."

"You know, I've always wanted you to hurry and get with someone. I don't mind who."

"That's a bit rude, don't you think?"

"James and I want to go on double dates, okay!" Poppy whined.

"Yeah, that's not happening any time soon, sorry."

"Can you just tell me one thing?"

"What?" Willa asked, curious as to where this was heading.

"Is he hot?" Poppy grinned devilishly.

"Poppy!"

"Sorry, sorry, I get it. It's your business."

"But yes. Very hot." Willa surprised herself with her words.

"I knew it!" Poppy shouted again, this time making customers look over at the commotion. Willa meekly sipped at her hot chocolate in response.

"So, are you seeing him again?"

"I'm not sure. It depends on if anything pops up with the project. It's strictly work between us." In the back of her mind, she wondered if strictly work buddies texted each other about exams results.

"Well, I'm very excited to see how this pans out," Poppy said sincerely.

"So am I," Willa mainly referred to the secret case.

"Oh! I almost forgot!" Poppy perked up, running back behind the counter. She bent down, looking into a few drawers, and then jumped back up again. She held her hands triumphantly in the air, and they were cradling something that Willa couldn't quite see.

"What is it?" Willa asked.

"The tickets came in the mail!"

"Tickets?"

"For The Bakery, obviously." Poppy rolled her eyes and ran back to their table. She carefully passed Willa the envelope as if it was a military-grade document.

"Oh, right! They arrived quite quickly, didn't they?"

"I have a friend who works the venue, and they popped in to give them to me this morning," she chirped.

"How much did they cost?" Willa reached for her wallet.

"Don't be silly." Poppy stopped her hand. "I got them for free. Another perk of having friends in high places."

"I need to make some friends like that," Willa said in awe.

"I think the Sheriff is in a pretty high place." Poppy winked.

"I swear to god, Poppy."

"That was the last joke, I promise!"

"Good. But in all seriousness, I'm so excited to see Luke Ross in his element," Willa said, referring to the dorky lead singer of The Bakery.

"Don't tell James, but I'm more of a fan of Ian Smith," Poppy blushed, referring to the drummer.

"Your secret's safe with me," Willa laughed, finishing her drink. "Well, I better get going. First, I need to email Annabel Hale an RSVP to her dinner."

"Oh, about that!" Poppy had a light bulb moment. "You should look online at some actual environmental firms, in case she agrees to give you a reference, or in case a member attends the dinner. I don't know. It's good to have some background information about the guests attending, anyway."

"Yeah, sounds good. I'll check it out." Willa said with a sincere smile, standing up in her seat and plucking the ticket from the table. "I'll see you later, Poppy."

"See you later." She smiled back.

"Oh, and say hi to James for me!" Willa added on her way out of the coffee shop.

"Say hi to Rome!" she heard Poppy call out from behind her.

Willa let out a noise that was a mixture of a groan and a chuckle, but continued the journey to her car. Maybe she would say hi to Rome for her. Or maybe not, Willa laughed.

***

Tonight was the first official night of the power cuts, and Willa was filled with anticipation. With a nervous shake in her knees and a wide grin on her face, she sat in her small combined kitchen and dining room. It was around 11:30pm, meaning there were only 30 more minutes left of electricity for the evening.

Willa had prepped her freezer with bags of ice that should last throughout the night, but she didn't really believe anything would defrost too quickly within the four-hour resource drought.

She wondered what it would be like when it turned midnight. Would it just be as if she turned her lights off? Would it be scary? No, surely not. Regardless, she was highly anticipating the moment.

While waiting around, Willa got bored. She'd been sitting at her table, twiddling her thumbs and drinking tea since 10pm. She reached into her black faux leather backpack and pulled out her laptop, figuring that she'd research the firms as Poppy suggested.

"Where to start..." Willa said aloud, bringing up her email invitation once more. When she RSVP'd earlier, she noticed Annabel's official network website linked at the bottom.

Being Annabel's number one fan, she didn't necessarily need to research much more about her. Willa could probably recite Annabel's life resumé if she got asked to. Hell, she'd probably do it for fun.

Opening up the website, Willa was fortunate to see many names of esteemed environmentalists and the companies they worked with, too.

"Veronica Kelp, who are you?" she wondered. She made a new tab and typed in the name, and impressive results popped up.

Veronica Kelp was another scientist who dabbled in journalism – she had Willa's dream job. Willa was sure that making some positive small talk with her at the dinner table would be advantageous.

Just in case, Willa jotted down some points to bring up in conversation. Based on the search results, Veronica was an avid supporter of science programs for children, yet she had none of her own. She appeared to have a knack for baking, and Willa knew this because she found a picture from five years in the past where Veronica won second place at a local bake-off. Lastly, Veronica owned a cute poodle named Milo.

Willa returned to Annabel's website and saw that the next person listed was a woman named Penelope Quinn. So, like she did with Veronica, Willa made another tab and typed Penelope's name into the search bar.

Though she didn't have a poodle named Milo and wasn't publicly a baker, Penelope was very open about her work on social media. She wasn't just a tree hugger in theory, but instead, in the most physical sense. Penelope worked on projects to stop deforestation and dedicated a lot of her time planting trees around the area. Willa was dumbstruck as she realised that the local Quinn Woods, home to a fun picnic park and a few random herds of deer, was named after Penelope Quinn. She helped plant every single tree in those woods over two decades ago.

After looking through a few more people, it was clear to Willa that she was a small, unimpressive lamb thrown into a den of career conquering lionesses at this party. However, despite everyone being impressive, Willa noticed another trend. Even though most of these women were married, all well into their 40s, none of them had children.

Of course, choosing not to procreate is an entirely personal decision, and Willa had supported many friends who've mentioned they didn't want children. But there was an identifiable trend, and that couldn't be ignored.

Then again, maybe it was entirely coincidental.

Willa leaned back and looked down at her list of conversational topics and key facts about people, and she felt a sense of pride.

"I should be a detective," she laughed, and then furrowed her brow. But wait, wasn't she already one? Sure, she didn't have rights to the actual title, but she was an investigator working with the police.

Willa checked the time, and it was only 11:45pm. She then looked at her phone, feeling a pang of guilt. It had been a few days since she had contact with Rome, and while she was warm and bored inside, Rome had been on the lookout these past few hours.

Making a face of uncertainty, she reached for her phone and found Rome's number on her contact list. Willa pressed the little phone symbol and began calling him.

In an utterly platonic way, of course. A simple courtesy check.

Willa cleared her throat, readying herself to talk, but Rome had already answered the call.

"Willa, are you sick?" Rome asked. His tone even sounded concerned, catching her off guard.

His low voice also surprised her. Sometimes he seems so flamboyant, she often forgot he was primarily considered rough.

"What? No, I'm fine."

"Oh, right? That's good then, I guess."

"How's the patrol going?" Willa changed the topic swiftly.

"It's been pretty uneventful, but it's not as boring as I thought it would be. No hoodlums yet."

"Hoodlums?"

"You know, riffraff."

"I know what hoodlums are, Rome, and no one these days says

64

'riffraff.'"

"I see – you were just judging me," Rome contemplated, sounding dramatic.

"Don't be silly," she defended.

"I appreciate you checking in, though. You could say I'm pretty flattered."

"You flatter easily, then."

He chuckled. "I actually don't."

"Hmm," she said, not knowing how to respond.

"What are you doing up so late, anyway?"

"I'm just researching some people from environmental firms," she answered.

"You could use our database at the precinct. Then, you'll know everything there is to know about them," he suggested.

"I don't think you're supposed to advertise or offer that kind of thing..."

"Who's going to fire me, the Sheriff?"

"Don't you have to answer to the people above you? Like from other districts?"

"I won't tell anyone if you won't," he said lowly.

Willa shivered, knowing that he wasn't even joking.

"I think I'll have to pass. My moral compass is too high for that," she joked in return, letting out a small yawn halfway through the sentence.

"Go to bed, Willa," he cooed.

"Huh?"

"I know you must be tired, so go get some rest, okay?"

"Am I that bad to talk to?"

"No, I really like talking to you."

Willa paused for a moment, not expecting the change of tone. "I'll go to sleep when the lights go off."

"Why wait?"

"I want to see what it'll be like. I don't know."

"It's literally just going to get dark, and you're going to have to use your phone light to find your bedroom," Rome said, shattering the illusion Willa had built.

She huffed. "Whatever."

"Alright, fine. Where are you right now?"

"In my apartment…?"

"Yeah, I got that much. I meant, which room are you in?" she could practically hear him roll his eyes through the phone.

"The kitchen."

"Where's the best view of the city from your apartment?"

"Um… my room, maybe? Why?"

"Alright – go there – now," he said, his voice breaking into a pant.

His breathlessness distracted her. "Are you running?"

"I'm trying to get up to a hill. Are you in your room yet?"

Willa stood up from her spot at the dining table and swiftly walked to her room. "Yes, I'm here now."

"Good. How much time do we have," he mumbled. "It's 11:59, one minute left."

"So, what're you planning?"

"We're going to watch the city shut down," he said simply.

"Well, that sounds chaotic," Willa laughed, opening up her curtains and looking out into the streets.

"Alright, I'll correct my phrase. We're going to watch the city shut down – together."

"That almost sounds romantic," Willa said, her face scrunching in slight disgust.

"Ten… Nine… Eight… Seven… Six…" Rome began counting down in a deep, steady voice, and Willa rested her head on the window.

"Five… Four… Three…" he continued.

"Two… One." Willa whispered over Rome's voice.

Suddenly, as if it were clockwork, the bright city lights went dark one by one. It was almost a calming rhythm.

"Wow," Rome mumbled.

More and more lights flicked off, and suddenly the city was dark and quiet. Lastly, her bedroom light shut off, surrounding her in blackness.

Rome broke the silence as if knowing the power was being drained closer and closer to the phone service towers.

"You still there?" he asked.

"Yeah?"

"Goodnight, Willa."

Before she could say another word, her phone beeped, alerting her that her phone connection had finally died out.

"Goodnight, Rome," she whispered. A thick feeling made her stomach churn as she moved away from the dark window. The chat left her feeling strangely giddy, and she noticed her tone towards him had gradually changed since their first unfortunate meeting. While that wouldn't normally concern her, she felt uneasy because of how much she was growing to trust him. Willa was a guarded woman by nature, only letting a few people into her life at a time. Yet somehow, Rome was barging his way into her mind more than she'd like to admit.

Chapter Eight

The following day, sunlight crept through the curtains and onto Willa's face, making her eyelids twitch in annoyance. Finally, she let out a hefty yawn and rolled around to face the other direction.

"Just a little longer..." she begged, as if the sun was going to listen to her request. Willa wasn't a morning person, but she had an unfortunate sleep cycle where if she woke even slightly, she couldn't go back to sleep.

"Why me?" Willa kicked her legs in frustration. She opened one eye, looked at the clock hanging on her wall, and saw that it was already nearing noon. Her muscles stiffened – she didn't expect such a late sleep in. She sat up, slid off her bed, and left the room.

Willa dragged her feet one-by-one through the small hallway to the kitchen, where she was greeted by a half-empty cup of tea sitting next to her computer that she left stranded in the blackout.

She sat in the same spot as the night before and tapped the space bar on her laptop.

"Only 10% charged... me too, buddy."

She opened up her internet browser and began clicking out of the tabs. She had all the information she needed written in her notepad. After three clicks of the little 'X' symbol, she stopped, and her mouth gaped. Suddenly, she was wide awake.

"What in the world…?"

The open tab was an article about Veronica Kelp just two weeks prior, posted on a local news website. However, it wasn't Veronica's piece that had struck Willa's interest… it was what was down in the bottom right corner of the page, titled 'Other Stories on this Day'. Here lay the plug line of another article, stating that a part of a developing neighbourhood had been wiped out.

'A small street struck down on the outskirts of Devonthorpe, 24 people dead in total.'

"24 people!" Willa shouted out in shock.

'The cause of death is unknown, and though local police units consider it an open case, higher authorities are pressuring to label the issue a freak accident.'

"So, Rome knew about this?"

After saying that aloud, Willa sighed. Of course the Sheriff would know about 24 people dying in the local area. The strangest part of the situation was that it was two weeks ago, and she hadn't heard a thing about such a devastating incident.

Immediately, she scrolled down to the bottom of the article. Here, she saw that there weren't many views on the article, regardless of such an important topic.

It was almost like it had been blocked from external view — no one could see it outside the official news site. That fact was weird enough, but it made little sense for two weeks to go by with no comments.

Willa re-read the article, but this time, she was bothered by the segment regarding the local police department. If he's treating it like an open case, Rome didn't believe it was a freak accident.

Suddenly, her heart quickened. All berating jokes aside, he was a genuine person, and she trusted his opinion. But did that mean there was a mass murderer around the area? If higher-ups are blocking it, the precinct no longer had the jurisdiction to pursue the topic.

Though in saying that, she knew she wouldn't be investigating it, anyway. Rome had specifically kept her out of the loop on this situation... but why?

She stood up, her curiosity getting the best of her once more. The sudden movement made her stomach realise she hadn't eaten anything, and a loud grumble sounded.

"This is not the time," Willa huffed and ran by the kitchen.

She grabbed a protein bar from the cupboard and shuffled around the bench, rummaging for her keys. She'd only collected those bars for the unlikely event that she would go to the gym, but she just substituted them for quick meals instead. Either way, she knew her lifestyle wasn't that healthy... But she was still alive, and 24 other people weren't.

After grasping her keys, she ran to her apartment door with a mirror next to it. Looking over her appearance, she was sporting a severe case of bed hair, a red baggy shirt that she got from a free event, and some terrifyingly '80s looking tracksuit pants. She quickly slid on her Birkenstock sandals, but that didn't improve the look.

Willa was going to see Rome in a similar pyjama state to when they first met. However, because this was business, she tried to push her unkempt image to the back of her mind. It was just Rome, after all.

Just Rome. Somehow saying 'just' before such an eccentric character's name sounded so wrong.

Without a second thought, she swung open her door, made her way down to the apartment parking lot, and drove over to the local police precinct.

***

Rome was watching the clock tick by. His eyes grew heavy, and he tried to distract himself by recounting the previous night's events.

By making his way up a hill to watch the spectacle with Willa, he had to run further and further away from his car. It wasn't that much of an issue, but it meant he had to voyage back with only a dodgy torch lighting his way. Safe to say, he didn't get home as early as he would've liked, but the bonding experience was definitely worth it.

Suddenly, a soft knock sounded on the door, getting his attention.

"Come in," he said, clearing his throat and wiping the smirk from his face.

The door opened, and Deputy Charlie slithered in meekly. His bald spot shone from the intense lighting in Rome's office, and he gathered his thoughts.

"What is it, Charlie?" Rome asked straightforwardly.

"Rome, well, you see…" he began, "My wife asked me to go meet her for a late lunch… and you know how she is."

Rome bowed his head, knowing he couldn't refuse. Francine was an intense woman, and he knew that he'd never hear the end of it if he got in the way of their impromptu date. Heck, last year he made the mistake of bringing Charlie in on their anniversary, and he had to hide from her wrath at the precinct Christmas party.

Rome shivered and then looked up again. He knew he had to let Charlie leave, but he was so tired. He didn't know if he could do all the work by himself in his current state, and he didn't want to get behind on administration when he had a time-sensitive case to work on.

"Yeah, of course, head home early," Rome smiled, and Charlie gushed with relief.

"Thanks. I'll make it up to you."

"Don't worry about it," Rome reassured, and Charlie left the room.

Suddenly, there was another knock at the door, however much more forceful than the first.

"Charlie, just go to lunch. It's okay!" Rome shouted out, but immediately the door opened, and without permission, Willa walked in.

71

"I'm not Charlie, as you can see," she said.

A smile made its way onto Rome's face, accidentally revealing that he was pleasantly surprised. Then he took in her appearance, and his smile grew wider.

Willa's cheeks were red and flushed, and she was wearing simple loungewear. Despite looking like she just got out of bed, her stance was stiff, and he could see a vein pulsing on her forehead. It reminded him of when he first saw her on the night of the supposed 'robbery' with Ron and Dave.

However, though she looked similar now to then, Rome couldn't think a bad thought about her. Maybe his original bias made him a bit judgemental the first time, when he thought Charlie had arrested a crazy thief… but now she was just endearing.

"Well, you look adorable."

"Oh, shut up," she quipped in distaste.

"To what do I owe the pleasure?" Rome grinned, sitting back in his chair.

She immediately grabbed out her phone, typed in a URL, and then marched towards his desk.

Willa was small and unassuming but could manage to appear intimidating at times. Because of this fact, Rome's heart quickened anxiously.

"What the hell is this?" she shouted, holding the phone in front of his face.

He gulped.

"How didn't I know about this? Why doesn't anyone know about this?" Willa pushed.

He sighed. "Look, Willa. That has nothing to do with this precinct anymore."

"Rome, 24 people died!" she exclaimed.

"Yes, I know. Who do you think had to help clean up the bodies?"

his eyes hardened.

She dropped her hand and let her guard down a bit, coming to terms with the situation. It was more than just a fact or just an article. Sure, she knew about the gravity of the deaths... but why was she getting angry at Rome?

"Okay, okay. That was pretty blunt. I'm sorry," Rome said, rubbing his face with his hands.

She squinted her eyes... Why was he apologising when she was at fault?

"I didn't tell you because there was no need to burden you with the details. But, as you can see, it's a pretty morbid topic. We had only just met, and you had just recently dealt with Joe.

"Also, I didn't intend for it to be a secret; I even talked to a few journalists. Usually it's their responsibility to spread the information, isn't it?" he added.

"I guess so," she uttered, feeling a tad guilty. Willa clearly directed her frustration at the wrong person. She sat down in a chair in front of him.

"I really don't know why it didn't go public, but I thought it had something to do with my superiors insisting it was an accident."

"Do you think they paid off the press to keep it quiet?" Willa asked.

"I guess, but it wasn't in my jurisdiction to investigate properly. The case is closed. People died, and it was sad, but what's happened has happened," he said.

Willa slumped down in a chair, feeling even more confused. "I was relying on you to give me some answers, Rome."

"Well, I'm sorry to disappoint you." He sighed, resting his head in his hand.

"Also, I'm sorry that I couldn't say goodnight last night," Willa mumbled.

"Was that seriously worrying you?" Rome asked, shocked.

"Well, no. But I just thought I'd say it," she said.

"Hmm, okay."

They sat in silence for a few seconds, but it wasn't awkward. Rome's eyes fluttered closed every now and then from being tired, and Willa sat staring at him.

"How did we just recover from an argument so easily?"

"Because we've got good intentions," he answered.

Her brow raised dubiously. "Okay, Doctor Know-It-All."

"Don't ask me a question if you're just going to tease my answer," he joked.

"Fine, I won't."

"I'm kidding; keep asking me anything you like," he said immediately.

He got up from his chair and walked over to a beaten-up, brown leather couch. He sat down on the far-left side, leaving Willa plenty of space to join him.

"So, after last night, do you think it's possible to catch the 'riffraff'?" Willa asked, referencing his words from their phone call.

"If all goes well, I think so. Our rotations were pretty smooth, and everyone cooperated well. The things people will do for some extra cash, am I right?" he chuckled, sinking into the couch, twiddling his fingers over the edge of the armrest.

"We're lucky that Arthur is paying for their extra work. Because, based on the lack of maintenance here, it seems like we're not granted much funding," Willa concluded, looking around.

"Maybe I like this style?"

"This style is the office equivalent of my current state, Rome." She laughed, pointing to her outfit.

"Good. I said earlier that I thought it was adorable."

Willa paused, realising that he might actually be serious.

She stood up and stretched, and Rome stood up too, ready to usher her out of the door — well, if that was where she was heading.

"Where's Charlie?" Willa asked.

"He went home early to have a date with his wife," Rome answered. He walked towards the door and began opening it for her.

"Are you asking me to leave?" she asked.

"What? Aren't you leaving?" he said, holding up his hands in retreat.

"I wasn't!"

"Then why did you stand up as if you were?"

"Maybe I was stretching my legs?"

"This happened last night, too. It feels weird when you call without a motive or sit and talk without a purpose," Rome defended, kicking his legs, emphasising the 'weird' feeling.

"Are you saying I make you uncomfortable?"

"Yes – wait – no. Well, now you are," he whinged.

"You're always messaging me asking about how I'm doing; I thought I'd be able to do the same?"

"You can!"

"Then, why is this conversation happening?"

"Because you're so inconsistent… and I'm also exhausted."

She squinted. "How am I inconsistent?"

"You're always talking lowly to me, and then you come in looking all cute with your angry, accusing face and suddenly be nice and apologise for not saying goodbye on the phone last night? How do I prepare for your crazy antics?"

"Pardon?"

"Alright, I'm rambling. I apologise. Once again, I'm exhausted."

"Then go to bed!" she directed, crossing her arms.

"I can't. I have to be here for another few hours at the least," he began. "I don't care about the paperwork anymore, but I'm not allowed to leave in case people call the office number instead of the emergency phone since we're technically supposed to be open."

Willa observed Rome for a few seconds and was reminded of her younger cousins when they were toddlers. He's a grown adult — and while they were both in their twenties, he was having a tantrum about a nap.

Rome began to run a hand through his hair out of stress, and Willa reached out, gently stopping him. Rome's eyes widened at the sudden contact and looked at her hand. His gaze made its way to her face, waiting for Willa to say something.

"I can stay around to answer phones if you want? My phone is fully charged for personality quizzes, and I have nothing else to do," she offered generously.

Rome's head tilted back, baring a relieved smile. He then took hold of the hand that stopped him.

"Because you owe me, you're going to do me this favour," he said, dragging her over to the couch and sitting her down on the far-right side.

"Are you seriously turning my grand, generous gesture into me paying back a debt? Why do I owe you?" she asked.

"Because I showed you such a sight last night."

"Anyone could've seen that!" Willa defended.

"Yes, but you were sitting in your kitchen, ignorantly away from the lightshow." He sat down beside her but faced his back in her direction.

He swung his legs up onto the couch, his knees hooking over the armrest because of his height. Rome then began lowering his back, ready to lie down with his head in her lap. Willa put her hands up, blocking him.

"What are you doing?" she quickly asked.

He turned his neck around, trying to see a glimpse of her face. "I'm claiming my debt."

"Aren't you crossing the line with workplace boundaries?"

"You said you'd help me sleep, didn't you?"

"I definitely did not. I meant that I'd let you sleep. On your own."

"Hmm, I don't think so," he tried to lie down again, and this time she didn't stop him. As he closed his eyes to rest, slight pain made its way to his forehead, and as he opened his eyes, he realised she had just flicked him. "Did you just assault a police officer?"

"How would you know? Your eyes were closed."

Rome couldn't argue with that one. He grasped onto the hand that rested on his chest. "Thanks for sticking around, Willa."

"You're saying a lot of gross things today, Rome."

"You know what? I guess I am." He brushed over her words, closing his eyes once again. Suddenly, another sensation could be felt, but it wasn't a flick on the forehead. Instead, Willa was lightly playing with his hair.

"Goodnight, Rome," she said finally, despite it being daytime.

As he kept hold of her hand, he kneaded her palm soothingly with his thumb. "Goodnight, Willa."

Realistically, Rome knew that he could wake up if a call came through. After all, the precinct phone volumes were designed to be loud. He wasn't really relying on Willa to stay awake or even stay around. But she did stay around.

And although there was the weight of Rome's heavy frame on her legs, and though she had an issue with going to sleep during the day, Willa's eyes also began to close, and she fell into a short slumber.

Chapter Nine

Rome's eyes creased and wrinkled, gaining the strength to open wide. He finally felt refreshed and ready to take on another night of guard duty. As he looked around, there was a sense of disorientation, as if he didn't remember where he was.

What confused him most of all was that he was staring up at Willa, who had fallen asleep also, resting her head back on the couch. For the first time since meeting her, he had the opportunity to properly observe her without her smart-ass commentary.

He chuckled, knowing how she'd act if he called her a smart-ass out loud.

As his chest vibrated, Willa began to stir in her sleep. Her head whipped forward, unbalanced, and Rome laid still with wide eyes.

Somehow, she didn't wake from that. Rome learnt in a short moment that Willa was quite a deep sleeper. But since her head dropped down, she was now angled to directly face him.

The sudden intimacy made his stomach flip, but he didn't want to inch away. His hand instinctively moved to her face, and he traced the curve of her jaw.

Despite their roles, and though it only started as deep curiosity, he couldn't help his attraction towards her. She was both intelligent and brave, something he admired.

But there was a sense of vulnerability – and staring up at her now, he realised how fragile she honestly looked.

Her body type was slim, and as his fingers traced down her arm, he could tell she didn't have a lot of muscle. Certainly not enough to go out investigating alone at midnight. Not only was he attracted to her personality, she was undeniably beautiful. She probably got a lot of attention from people her age, and he couldn't blame them.

Interrupting his train of thought, the office phone began ringing, and he tried his best not to jolt in surprise. Instead, Rome tensed his abdomen and raised himself off of Willa's lap, using his hands to place her head back down on the chair gently.

While manoeuvring her, Willa's eyes opened wide, and as he held her face, she was startled.

"What are you doing?" she croaked.

"Ah, sorry, I'm just getting up to get the phone," Rome spoke awkwardly, removing his hands and twisting off the couch with a step.

"…Right," Willa mumbled, noticing the ringing in the background.

As Rome stood tall behind his desk, taking the phone off the hook, Willa squinted her eyes, focusing on his bed hair.

Willa frowned, wondering how he still managed to look picturesque. She licked her dry lips and found hardened drool down her chin. There was quite a contrast between the two.

Wiping it off quickly, she turned her mind to Rome's phone call in an attempt to hide her embarrassment.

His forehead creased as he coiled the phone cord around his fingers, only saying some short mumbles in response.

"Right… Yeah… I'll be there soon…" he uttered, putting the phone back on the hook.

"Everything okay?" she asked, rising from the chair.

"Arthur says something feels a bit fishy down at one of the sites… I think I better take a look."

"Did you need any help?"

"Nah, I don't want you going near it. So please, make it home safely," he stated, walking to the door and holding it open.

"Seriously?" she huffed.

"These were the terms, Willa," he reminded.

"Right, okay. Let me know how it goes," she replied, following his direction.

"I'll call you tonight."

"Good," Willa said, stopping her strides.

Good?

"Wait, don't call if it isn't urgent," she recovered, keeping her calm facade.

He chuckled, shutting the door behind her. "Typical."

Grabbing his keys and buckling on his holster, he ran to his police car and sped away in a hurry. Arthur had directed him to the circuits on Joyce street, where apparently Arthur noticed some surges from afar. It was already getting dark, so it was about time that he made his way over to guard the area, anyway.

Despite being prepared for the evening's shift, Rome's heartbeat quickened in pace as he neared the scene. Then, he slowed his car down and parked out of sight so that he could catch people in the act.

Like every regular human in the face of a potential threat – apart from maybe Willa – he swallowed dryly, feeling a little too nervous. As he softly shut his car door behind him, he gripped his waist, double-checking that he had his gun in his holster.

Rome stepped over to the circuit area on Joyce street and noticed it was empty.

There were no signs of tampering so far and not a single person in sight. He sighed, not knowing whether it was too early to feel relieved or not.

He grabbed his phone out and dialled Arthur's number to see if there was any extra information.

"Hello?"

"Hey, it's me. I'm on Joyce street," Rome informed.

"Has it already been tampered with?" Arthur asked.

"No, nothing yet. Are you sure this was the site with surges on it?" Rome asked, breathing out cool air as he peered around.

"Yeah, I'm sure… It matched the pattern like all the other times."

"Hmm, funny," Rome wondered, feeling an ounce of confusion.

"Do you need any help over there?" Arthur asked, feeling eerie.

"No, it should be fine. It's empty, after all."

"Right, well, call me if you find anything else," Arthur prompted.

"Will do. Catch you later, Art," Rome said, pulling the phone away to end the call.

Suddenly, he heard some rustling nearby, and his ears pricked up. He brought out his flashlight and shone it in the direction of the noise.

"Hello?" Rome prompted, squinting his eyes.

There was no answer, and his heart thumped faster.

As his eyes focused on a nearby bush, he saw movement, and behind the branches, Rome made out a figure. They emerged from their crouching position and he could see that they hid behind a mask. A white one with a light-hearted pointy nose and a permanent dark grin. It was the type of mask that wouldn't be scary enough for a Halloween costume, but seeing it on the face of someone at a crime scene? Rome was a short second away from being terrified.

"Police! Who's there?" Rome called, placing his hand on his gun.

The person in the mask walked forward without uttering a word.

"Hey, stay where you are!" Rome called out.

They crept forward again, taunting his resolve, and Rome unholstered his gun. "I'm warning you, stop moving and speak up!" he called again, pointing the gun at him.

The person froze and put their hands up slowly, before shifting their head's angle to see past Rome.

Was he looking at the gun?

Rome looked in the direction quickly and saw another masked person, just a foot behind him.

"What the—"

Suddenly, something swung toward him, and with one forceful blow to the head, he dropped to the ground.

He started drifting into an unconscious state as he watched the two masked people hover over him. The one from the bush looked up at the other, who was holding a crowbar.

"Fuck," Rome exhaled as darkness overtook his vision.

***

Rome shivered, and it dawned on him that he was far too underdressed for the dry winter air. He scrunched his eyes tighter, trying to sleep through it, but he wasn't just bothered by the cold; it seemed he had a raging headache, too.

"I didn't go drinking last night, did I?" Rome groaned, remembering the last time he had to rock up to work with a hangover. It certainly wasn't a day he'd like to repeat, that's for sure. Soon, a cool wind danced over his clothes, causing him to shiver once more. As he came to, he knew something wasn't right. He never kept his window open… so why was there a breeze?

His eyes struggled to open, but when they did, all he could see was the galaxy above. Rome loved stargazing, but why was he sleeping under them now? He strained his muscles and sat up, his head rushing as he peered around. It was still night, but as his eyes darted around, he pieced together what happened. There was a street sign that read Joyce street; there was his police car parked in the distance, and only a few metres away was an unburied, opened, and tampered set of cables.

Rome gulped, nervous about assessing the damage he knew was there. His right hand reached the back of his head, and he winced at the wet consistency. He used his free hand to grab his torchlight and shone it over his fingers. As he guessed, he was bleeding – a lot.

Rome groaned, feeling a loss of energy, before reaching into his pocket and grabbing out his phone. He'd missed eight missed calls from Arthur, so Rome dialled back immediately.

"Hey, Arthur? Yeah, they took over Joyce street."

Chapter Ten

Willa looked out her window to the city lights, before turning her attention to her phone's lock screen. She was waiting for Rome's call, but she didn't know why she was so expectant of it in the first place.

Maybe it was because she hated people who didn't keep their word and not because she actually wanted to talk to him. That wasn't possible.

She stared up at the roof with a sigh and debated checking her phone once more, even though she knew there'd be no notification.

As if the god of distractions granted her wish, her door buzzed, alerting a visitor.

Her eyes peeked up to the clock on her wall, and she frowned.

Who was visiting her at 2am?

Wait, why was she even up at 2am?

With quick momentum, she heaved herself out of bed and tiptoed towards her door. She looked forward into the keyhole with caution, feeling she should find out who was there before opening.

As she pushed her face to the door, she felt a sense of disbelief.

"Rome?"

"Hey..." he said, looking flat.

"What are you doing here?" she frowned.

"Willa... I, I need your help," he stuttered, stumbling forwards.

Willa stood up to catch him as best she could, but her tiny frame could only hold so much weight. What on Earth was wrong with him?

His head rested on her shoulder, and her hand went to stroke the back of it. But as she heard Rome's breath hitch, she pulled her hand back away. "Rome?"

He sighed, lacking the energy to explain and instead leaned down to show her his head wound. His hair was dripping with red, and it didn't take long for Willa to understand the situation.

"Shit, Rome!" she called out, ushering him inside with a quick pace.

She plonked him down on a chair and gripped his chin. As she looked into his eyes, panic overcame her. "Rome, what happened?"

"I, uh, I got attacked at the site."

"What should we do? Should I call an ambulance?" Willa panicked, grabbing out her phone.

"No, no, I'll be fine," he muffled.

"Rome, you're practically bleeding on my couch," Willa warned.

"Really? It's that bad?" he mumbled, feeling weaker by the second.

"We need to get your wound fixed. Let's go," she called, readying herself to stand.

"Can't you stitch me up?" he asked.

"Don't be stupid," she said, standing up. Willa tried to hide her concern, but her knees felt like jelly at the idea that he was being serious.

"Willa… I need your help, now," he croaked, feeling slightly scared.

"Frick…" she gently brushed his hand away. "One moment, I'll grab the first aid kit."

By no means was Willa a professional when it came to stitching someone up, but she had no choice. The way Rome looked now proved that he needed some urgent first-response care, and she was the best he had.

Willa reached for the kit from under her bed and quickly returned to the lounge room. Pulling out her phone, she picked the first YouTube tutorial with a decent-looking thumbnail and sat beside Rome.

"This looks like it will hurt... I'm sorry," she warned, then got to work.

After five minutes worth of audible wincing from both Willa and Rome, the bleeding halted. Somehow, Willa managed to seal it up enough for Rome to get it looked at in the morning.

"How does it look?" he asked, feeling more alert with some pain killers in his system.

"I don't think we should be too picky on the aesthetics, given the circumstance, but it's much better than I expected," she said, gently rustling his hair to inspect it.

"That's fine. My hair will cover it anyway," he said, tilting his head to rest on her shoulder. Since the office nap earlier, Willa didn't need to pull away from the new normal.

"What happened?" she asked again.

"People in masks... they attacked me with a crowbar," he shivered as he remembered the scene.

"Shit, Rome..."

"They're more dangerous than I expected them to be," he said.

"We'll need more volunteers," she said. "You can't have people doing guard shifts alone anymore."

"I know, I thought the same."

"Did you notice anything? Did you recognise a voice? Anything at all?" Willa interrogated, tucking her legs underneath her as she sat back on the couch.

He sighed. "No, no, and no."

"Also, why did you come here?"

"I needed help."

"You should've gone to the hospital, Rome," she lectured.

"Nah, you did a good enough job," he chuckled.

"Rome, this isn't a joke. What if I didn't answer the door? Could you imagine if I left the apartment tomorrow and found you dead on my doorstep?"

He smirked. "Would you cry?"

"I would've been royally pissed off."

"Ah, I guess that's something," he said, turning his body around to face her.

"Are you feeling better?" she asked, referring to his sudden energy boost.

"A little, thank you," he said, reaching out towards her.

"What are you doing?" she said, leaning backward.

He looked up at her face, then down to her side. "Can't I hold your hand?" he asked, raising his brow.

"I mean… sure, but I don't know why you want to," she hesitated.

"Eh, I have my reasons," he said, feeling unsure of himself as well.

"Did you want me to call you a taxi home? Do you think you'll be okay?" she asked.

"Is it alright if I crash here?" he tapped his hand over the couch.

"In your current state, that's probably a good idea. I'll grab some blankets for you," she said, swiping his hand away as she stepped up.

"Right, thank you."

When she returned, Rome was already sleeping, letting out a soft snore from his seated position.

Willa sighed, wondering what sort of mess she'd gotten herself into, before placing the blanket gently on him and walking back to her own room. She didn't know if he should even be sleeping at this point, especially with a concussion of sorts. She was too tired to think of the risks because her head was already filled with selfish worry.

He almost died tonight because of the case, and that meant she'd placed herself in danger twice now. Willa shivered at the thought. She shut her bedroom door and retreated to her bed for some well-needed rest.

***

For the second time in the past 24-hour period, Rome woke with the feeling of a raging hangover... Except this time, he was well aware of why.

He opened his eyes and peered around the room, collecting his bearings. Finally, he sat up and let out a yawn, catching the moment Willa walked into the room.

She was wearing a baggy t-shirt and a pair of tights underneath, with her hair wrapped up in a towel.

"Oh, you're up? I made you breakfast," she chirped.

A grin took over his face, and he cautiously stood from the couch, trying hard to avoid a head rush.

"Good morning," he said, walking over to her kitchen bench.

"Good? Maybe an overstatement, given last night," she said, passing Rome a glass of water and two pain killers.

"Drugging me up so early?" he asked, taking the water.

"Oh? Sorry, I thought your head might be hurting still," she said, attempting to close her hand that held the pills.

Rome eagerly snatched them back before she put them away.

"Are you feeling any better?" she asked.

"Yeah, but I'll still get a check-up when the doctors open," he said, looking at the time on his watch.

"Good plan." She sat down next to him.

As Rome finished his eggs on toast, his eyes fell into a daze. When he blinked, he could see the people in their masks, watching him as he bled out on the ground.

"What's up?" she asked, catching his attention again.

He shook his head, regaining his focus.

"Will you come to the doctors with me?" Rome asked.

"Sorry, why? You're a grown adult, Rome."

"Do me a favour, Willa."

Her brows raised. Hadn't she done enough? But instead of complaining, she thought up a different excuse.

"They're just going to judge my stitch-work, and I don't think I can handle that," she said with a grimace.

"Oh, hush, when have you ever cared what other people think?"

She rolled her eyes. "All the time, I just don't vocalise it like you do."

Rome left space for an awkward pause, knowing she'd want to fill it.

"Fine, I'll go to the doctors," she said, standing up to get ready.

Rome grinned with a sense of accomplishment, then cleared their plates and gathered his things.

Willa insisted on driving, and when he told her where to go, it seemed Rome went to the same medical centre that she frequented.

The pair got out of the car and greeted Toby, the front desk receptionist, who gave them permission to walk straight through.

Apparently, the town's Sheriff didn't have to bother with a waiting time, unlike everyone else.

Willa followed Rome to the same doctor's office that she was so familiar with. She felt suddenly uncomfortable with the idea that not only did they share so much in common, but now she was about to witness a rather personal affair.

Rome knocked his annoying knock, and they entered the room.

"Rome, Willa?" Dr. Whitman greeted, surprised by the unlikely duo.

"Wait, you know her?" Rome asked.

"She's also my patient," he answered.

"Ah, I see."

Willa nodded politely but stayed in a shy, quiet state.

"So, how can I help you today, Rome?" Dr. Whitman asked.

"Well, I got hit by a crowbar last night, and I think it split my head open a little," Rome stated in the most nonchalant way possible.

"...Right, well, I'll definitely have to take a look at that," he said, standing up and stepping forwards.

He tousled through Rome's hair momentarily before coming to a halt. "It's already stitched?"

"Ah, Willa gave it her best shot," Rome stated.

"Willa? Really?" Dr. Whitman looked over to her.

"Sorry, I did my best, but it probably complicated things, didn't it?"

"Not at all. You've done a great job." He dropped his hands and stepped away from Rome.

"See? Willa, I knew you did well," Rome spoke aloud.

"I didn't know you were interested in medicine," Dr. Whitman stated to her.

"I'm not, well, it's not that I don't like the profession – I mean, it was just a fluke," she muttered.

He smiled at her response. "Well, I'm impressed, nonetheless. You must have a steady hand."

Rome frowned, disliking that the attention had shifted away from himself.

"Oh, don't be silly," she blushed, feeling proud.

If there was one thing people knew about Willa, she was a bit of a suck-up to industry professionals. She became coy and modest while giving praise back to the other like a mirror.

"Maybe you should swap degrees," Dr. Whitman joked.

She laughed. "I graduate next month, so I think that would be the worst decision ever."

"You graduate next month? Congratulations, I didn't know," he grinned.

Rome scrunched up his face further as the conversation progressed and turned around to them.

"So, do I need anything done?" Rome interrupted in an attempt to bring them both back.

"Oh, right," Dr. Whitman said, returning to his chair. "I'll write you a script for some stronger pain killers, but as far as structural revival, Willa's stitch job is really all you needed."

"Seriously?" Rome heard Willa gasp from behind and he felt the need to interrupt again.

"Well, in that case, we better go. We've got lots of work to do, don't we, Willa?" he turned his head to her.

"Well, I guess so?"

"Alright, here's your script," Dr. Whitman said, handing it to Rome. "You both take care now."

"Will do," Rome said, walking himself out.

"Thanks, Dr. Whitman," Willa chirped.

"Just call me Barry, Willa," he replied.

Rome frowned again.

"Alright, see you later, Barry."

The pair walked out of the doctor's office, and Rome paused, folding his arms.

"You're pretty chummy with your GP," he stated.

"Oh, shut up, Rome."

Chapter Eleven

I t had officially been a week since Willa took Rome to the doctors, and things had been strangely quiet.

Sure, Rome managed to find an excuse to call her every couple of days, but there was no progress on the case, and therefore no real reason for them to be speaking.

When they did talk, he'd fumble around the topic of Dr Whitman, out of almost misplaced jealousy. It irked her completely, not to mention that any insinuation would make her next doctor's appointment uncomfortable.

Willa took a deep breath, in and out, and turned her car radio up.

Today was the day of the golden dinner. She needed to have a clear head if she wanted to impress the elite Annabel Hale, Veronica Kelp and Penelope Quinn.

After an uneventful week, Willa should have been able to focus on preparing herself for the evening. Still, she was a little preoccupied worrying about Rome's attack.

Hit by a crowbar… if they were hostile to that level, who knew how far they could go. But more importantly, why was their mission worth that level of violence? Willa had so many unanswered questions, and she worried she'd never get closure.

Trying to stop her mind from wandering again, she focused on her surroundings.

According to the GPS, Willa was about 20 minutes away from her destination, aka, away from Annabel Hale's house. As she got closer, the houses looked nicer and nicer, making Willa feel a bit out of her depth.

Though the area was getting richer, it surprised Willa to see the traffic thickening. As she approached the next suburb, she noticed her estimated arrival time was later than before.

A traffic jam? At this time? Perhaps there was a special event, Willa wondered. Otherwise, based on how far out of the city they were, it made no sense.

The car crept on at a slow pace, and Willa looked out to see a line of police cars parked along the side of the road.

If she squinted hard enough, she was sure she'd see Rome there, too. But it wasn't just his precinct involved; it couldn't be. There were over eight cars lined up, and Rome had three accessible cars on a good day.

She rolled on closer.

Willa could now see an ambulance fleet parked further inwards, hidden by the police cars. There were five of them – what could have needed five ambulances? Willa suddenly remembered the mass death from two weeks ago. Could it be related?

Surely not, Willa thought. But really, she was far from being sure.

Her heartbeat quickened its pace, and she reached for her phone. Yes, she shouldn't reach for a phone while driving, and especially when driving past eight police cars, but she wanted to get to the bottom of this.

She dialled Rome's number expecting an immediate answer.

But the phone rang, and rang, and rang until she reached his message bank.

"That's strange," Willa mumbled.

She pressed his number again, clearing her throat as she readied herself for an answer, but instead, the dial rang out once more.

An uncomfortable feeling washed over her. He's there for sure, and if he's not answering leisurely, something must have gone wrong.

Or maybe he just didn't want to answer her call?

After all, she'd been acting irritated around him recently… it would only make sense that he'd want to drift away. Willa cringed, hating her feeling of entitlement. He was free to call or not call whoever he pleased. She shouldn't care.

The cars ahead started to pick up speed, and her GPS finally began knocking the minutes down.

Willa soon arrived at a gate plated in gold, revealing a concrete house behind it. The whole area featured mix and match decorations, but it somehow blended together to create a vision of class.

Willa parked on the side of the road, to the left of the gate. When she walked to the entrance, she pressed the button on the intercom.

"Willa Triston?" an older man's voice spoke.

"Yes, that's me," Willa answered

"Make your way inside," he said, and the gates opened automatically.

She stepped inside what appeared to be a fairy wonderland. It was an overgrown garden, with vines bordering the walkway and a sea of green, speckled with random white flowers decorating the space. Willa could see butterflies settling on top of the flowers, nearly hidden by the long grass around them – but the garden wasn't overgrown in an unkempt way. It was shaped well, with the sole intention of flourishing biodiversity.

Willa made a mental note of the arrangements, hoping to adopt Annabel's style in the future when she could afford her own yard.

As she approached the front door, it opened inwards before she could grab the handle. A greying man stood by the entrance.

"Willa," he greeted.

It was the same voice from the gate. Willa had never been to a house with a butler before, and honestly, she didn't feel like it was Annabel's style. But of course, what would she know.

"My name is Gerald. Come on through."

The wall behind where he stood displayed a giant glass feature, spanning from the floor to the ceiling. Preserved in the glass, there were at least a hundred butterflies pinned down as if they were stuck in a science lab. For a moment, Willa felt unsettled. After seeing the butterflies flying freely outside, this sudden contrast was almost menacing. But Annabel was a famed scientist, and her interest in pinning was just part of the gig.

Willa followed Gerald through the minimalistic house and ended at a grand dining room. The 12-seater table was filled with 10 esteemed environmentalists. The extra chairs held space for her and Annabel Hale, who stood by a wide, open window. At Willa's arrival, the room stopped their chatting, and Annabel caught on.

She swiftly moved her head to the side, acknowledging Willa's presence with a broad, white-toothed smile.

"Willa, you've arrived!" she spoke with sudden familiarity.

"Hi, everyone," Willa smiled coyly.

Annabel walked over to Willa, ushering her into the empty chair next to the head of the table.

"Sit, sit. We're all so excited to get started," she said.

"Sorry, was I late?" Willa asked, knowing everyone had arrived much earlier than she did. Sure, traffic was terrible, but Willa was prepared for this and left home ahead of schedule. She arrived on time regardless.

The man sitting in the seat to the left of Willa leaned forward with a gushing smile.

"Late? Not at all, my darling. We were just so anxious to meet you," he said.

"Oh, you flatter me," Willa blushed.

"I'm Xavier, and this is my partner, Florence," he said, pointing to the lady next to him.

"Lovely to meet you both," Willa said.

"Likewise," Florence piped in.

"So, how was the drive over?" Annabel asked, still standing.

"Ah, it was fine… Actually, there was a bit of traffic, but it was manageable," Willa said.

"Traffic? Why do you think that might be?" she asked.

The room quietened down once more, and everyone turned to hear Willa's response.

"Well, there must have been an incident at the next suburb over. It looked like it was pretty intense, too," Willa explained.

"Oh? Well, I hope it wasn't that bad," Annabel seemingly dismissed further discussion and walked over to the window.

She opened the shutters, and with a breeze, a distinct smell wafted through the air. Willa recognised the scent, but she couldn't exactly tell from where. Annabel tipped her head back and breathed it in with a grin.

"Doesn't it just smell delicious?" Annabel asked, turning around.

"Absolutely," Xavier beamed.

Despite their praise, Willa couldn't understand the allure. The smell definitely didn't carry a flavour she'd think she wanted to try, but she still recognised it from somewhere. A charred scent carried alongside it, making her wonder if it was a burnt barbecue.

Dinner must almost be ready, then, Willa thought. As if on cue, Annabel floated over to the table and took her seat.

Small talk buzzed around the room, and Willa tried her best to keep up. Veronica and Penelope were the prominent guests she studied, but they were seated over the other end of the table. Luckily enough, Xavier and Florence were wonderful company, and Annabel piped in every now and then, too.

"Well, while we wait for the food to arrive, let us give an honorary introduction to our esteemed guest today," Annabel said. The guests followed her lead, giving Willa small applause.

As if on cue, Gerald and some caterers walked in with their meals. Unlike Willa's expectation of burnt meat, an array of salads and vegetable-based meals were placed on the table as Annabel continued to speak.

Of course – they were vegetarians. Her nose must not have been as accurate as she initially thought.

"I'm sure Willa already knows why she deserves a place at our table here today, isn't that right?" she asked.

"Well, actually, I'm not really sure what earned me this privilege," Willa admitted.

"Come now, no need to be modest, Willa," Xavier cooed.

"I'm serious," Willa said, not wanting to say her result was a fluke.

"Willa, your paper was superb," Annabel said.

"Well, why don't you remind us of what you wrote about?" Penelope's voice carried from the end of the table.

Willa took deep breath, feeling somewhat unconfident, but she knew to push through.

"Um, well, we were supposed to show how butterflies could balance an ecosystem, right?" she filled in the group.

"It was a simple act of pest control. I thought about it for a while, since they often resort to camouflage... but when butterflies or caterpillars are at risk of being eaten by ants, they turn against them and eat their larvae. If we got involved, we could use butterflies to our advantage – removing their threats and controlling ant population at the same time.

"Looking back, it probably isn't the best idea to control and minimise an existing species." Willa began to chuckle but realised no one followed along.

"And why is that a bad idea?" Penelope asked.

"Well, as a start, nature has a way of balancing itself out. We'd never want to cull a native population – think of the consequences," Willa squinted her eyes, wondering if this was the answer they wanted to hear.

"Of course not," Annabel smiled. "Dig in, everyone. You don't want your food to get cold."

***

Rome opened the door to his house, took off his jacket, and made a beeline towards the bathroom. He knelt beside the toilet bowl and gagged until his lunch came up. Safe to say, it hadn't been a good day.

He undressed and stepped into the shower, ran the hot water, and stood still. His nose flared until the stench washed from his hair and he finally turned off the water.

It wasn't the smell of vomit that bothered him, but the scent of death and the reminder of how many bodies he saw that day.

Rome walked to his room wearing a pair of dark grey pyjamas and flopped down on his bed. After charging for over 10 minutes, his phone finally came to light.

His pounding heart calmed before speeding up again, as there were three missed calls from Willa, accompanied by two additional messages.

W: How are things?

W: Call me if you get a chance.

He unlocked his phone with a quick swipe and returned her call.

"Hello?" Willa's voice came through.

"Hey, are you alright?" Rome asked.

"Yeah, I'm fine. Why?"

"Three missed calls from you feels a bit unreal. I thought you were kidnapped or something."

"Yeah, I totally could've been," she paused. "Are you okay?"

"Me? I'm fine, dandy, fantastic," he dismissed the question.

"...Right."

"What did you get up to today?" he asked.

"I had my dinner with Annabel Hale, actually."

He shot upwards into a sitting position. "Really? How'd it go?"

"It was good, a bit strange, but really good."

He laughed. "What do you mean by strange?"

"I don't know if I understand their humour, or maybe they don't get mine. It was fine, but I guess I'm a bit too used to your type."

He laid back with a grin. "My type?"

"Aloof, annoying, occasionally humorous," she teased.

He jokingly sucked air through his teeth as if wincing through the phone.

"Too far?" she asked.

"Willa, I need to see you."

"Is everything okay? Did something happen with the case?" she asked hurriedly.

He stared up at the ceiling, waiting for a response. "Did you really only want to see me for the case?"

"That's like it always has been, right?" Willa asked.

"It doesn't have to be."

"...I think you're a bit tired from your day, Rome."

"Maybe. Why don't I see you tomorrow, then?"

"Hmm?"

"It's the weekend. Let's do something."

Willa paused, unsure of what he was asking, and Rome's head suddenly filled with noise.

"...Well, sure," she answered.

His posture straightened. "Wait – really?"

"I don't see why not. I haven't got any other plans, and plus, I'm still riding the high from Annabel's dinner," she said.

He thought back to when they met after she first got her test results. It seemed every time Annabel was around Willa, it made it much easier to get along with her.

Thank you, Annabel, he thought.

"Well, I guess I'll pick you up tomorrow then?"

"Just tell me where you want to go, and I'll drive myself," she said stubbornly.

"I'll see you tomorrow," he ignored her statement, earning a groan from her. "Goodnight, Willa."

He expected her to hang up, but her voice sounded through the phone again.

"Hey, Rome?"

"Yeah?"

"Sleep well, okay. Try not to let work bring you down, no matter how hard it can be."

He looked at the phone in his hand and began to think back to what he'd said to her that day. She couldn't have known about what happened. Surely.

"Um, you too, Willa," he answered, hearing the phone line die afterwards.

***

Willa wore an uneasy feeling and couldn't tell if it was butterflies or anxiety. By the time 11am rolled around, Willa was dressed in a shorts and shirt combo, paired with some black over-sized sunglasses. Rome had messaged Willa in advance to tell her they'd be going on a pleasant stroll near a river, and this simple, breezy outfit was the closest she'd get to sporting activewear in public.

Right on time, her phone buzzed, meaning Rome was outside. She grabbed her purse and rode the elevator until she hit the ground floor. Standing at the glass door of her apartment complex, she peered outside.

Rome stood next to his trademark police car, wearing a similar ensemble to hers, except this time in a black shirt and shorts, paired by some wayfarers. She'd never seen him look so casual, and wearing black was a new colour for him. It suited him.

She opened the door and caught his attention, earning a toothy grin. "Good morning, Willa."

"We match," Willa stated, pointing back and forth between them.

"We do, don't we," he smiled, waiting for her approach.

"So, where exactly are we going?" she pushed her way past him, getting into the car. He followed her lead.

"Have you ever been to Lake Devonthorpe?" he asked.

"I only moved to the city to study, so I'm not familiar with every nook and cranny."

"It's past the outskirts, that's all the description you'll get." He started the engine and took off into the street.

Towards the end of the long drive, Willa could see that they were surrounded by forestry. Finally, the car pulled into an unmarked driveway where the sky was covered by a dark canopy. Soon, the car came to a halt.

Willa turned over to Rome with a straight face. "Is this where I die?"

"Just follow me," he teased, hopping out of the car.

She followed his lead into the deep, dark forest, trying to not feel too uncomfortable. Willa wasn't scared of the dark; she usually loved it. But no one liked an eerie forest when you're on alert – and since it'd been a while, her nerves about seeing Rome had gotten the better of her, even if she could trust him completely.

Willa could now see the clearing of trees ahead, where the sun streamed onto a glistening shoreline. As the duo got closer, she thought that the word 'lake' was a bit out of place, especially to be named after the town. It was a creek at best, but that didn't bother them.

Rome ushered Willa along the shoreline for a few minutes until some beach chairs came into view.

"This is us," Rome said, sitting down and kicking his feet out with relief.

"And what exactly are we doing here?" Willa asked, looking around. Rome didn't seem like the type to enjoy fishing, and there weren't any rods in sight, so why the creek?

"Take a seat," he pointed at the chair beside him. Willa followed his direction.

"So?"

"We're just going to sit and relax in the sun," he gleamed, stretching out again as if it were the hottest summer day.

"And that's it?" Willa asked, seemingly impatient.

"Oh, forgive me," he said as if he remembered something. He stood up and ran to the nearby tree line. Willa watched him pick up a box that he brought back with him.

"What's that?"

"Some reading material for our basking," he said.

Willa wondered what on earth would be inside the box in terms of what Rome considered reading material, but she was pleasantly surprised when he tipped it into her view. As expected, she saw crime novels and autobiographies. But to her delight, there was also a fair section filled with fantasy, comedy and classic romance.

"After you," he said, gesturing for her to pick one.

"Thank you," she said, choosing the cheesiest looking romance option and placing it on her lap after reading the blurb. Willa wondered if

Rome had read this one himself, or if he just collected it.

"Ah, good choice. A personal favourite," he said with sincerity, and Willa had to hold back a sexist chuckle.

Well, that answers it, she thought.

Rome sat once again, shuffling through the box for something that caught his eye. He pulled out a space-fantasy novel.

They sat reading, and the only sound heard was the soft flipping of pages and the sweet flow of the stream. It was calming, and she found herself enjoying the time that passed by. Then, after a long while, Willa noticed that Rome's page-turning had stopped, and he was looking up at her.

"You really are pretty," he said, challenging her peace and tranquillity.

"Where'd that come from?" she rolled her eyes.

"I have to ask you something, Willa," he said. His words building anticipation.

"What?" Willa asked nervously, looking down at her book.

"How did you know about work yesterday?"

"Pardon?" Willa turned back.

"You said on the phone that I shouldn't mind what happened," he explained.

"I was just speaking generally."

"Given the circumstances, it seemed motivated."

She tilted her head. "Are you interrogating me, Sheriff?"

"I just think you know more than you let on," he observed her.

Willa couldn't help but wonder why she felt a sudden disappointment. He was a detective, first and foremost. Of course, the relaxing day out wouldn't last forever, but what made him want to paint her out to be dishonest? And why, after calling her pretty so suddenly?

"When I was driving to Annabel's dinner, I saw police cars and ambulances pooled a few suburbs over, okay?" she huffed defensively.

"I see."

She sighed. "Why is it so wrong for me to know what's going on, Rome?"

His demeanour changed, and suddenly the bright man was sullen, as if begging Willa not to continue. Even if Rome started the conversation, he wasn't prepared to end it today. There was a thick silence, and it felt odd as Willa realised he was setting boundaries. But she couldn't blame Rome for being cautious.

Willa put her book to the side, preparing herself to do the only distraction technique she knew he'd fall for – flirtation. "So, you think I'm pretty?"

He smirked, looking down. The closeness between their chair placement was enough for their legs to be touching, and his feet inched nearer before retracting again.

The wind picked up, and suddenly water droplets started to tickle Willa's skin. It was starting to rain.

"Well, I think we better go home," he said, and so they did.

Chapter Twelve

It was 30 minutes before Rome's alarm went off, and while he was asleep, he was in an agitated state. Rome always found he was significantly tired whenever this happened, though it didn't happen often.

Rome was a vivid dreamer – and he found it draining. After all, he saw a lot of dangerous things at work, some that would traumatise most. It only made sense that he'd revisit those moments as his mind ventured about.

However, this time, it wasn't a dream about action-filled police chases, threats, or dead bodies. Instead, it was about Willa, and he couldn't tell if it was more or less tiring than the others.

The worst part about his vivid dreaming was that he'd often think everything was real. Then, if it was a good dream, he would wake to either a state of disappointment or disorientation.

In his dream, they were on the way to the lake, deep in the forest. He watched her walk ahead, hopping around each tree branch on the ground and crunching every leaf she could.

They were chatting about nothing at all. It was somewhat incoherent, like a mirage of conversation, but Rome quickened his pace. She turned around and stared into his eyes before stepping towards him.

Rome reached out his hand and felt the skin on her cheek. She smiled, and he leaned forward. When their lips finally touched, his eyes darted open, and he was pulled back to reality.

Beep, beep, beep.

Rome groaned, reaching over to his phone alarm and pressing the stop button.

"Well," he said out loud, feeling the unnecessary need to excuse his thoughts.

He got up, put his suit and badge on, and headed to the office.

Charlie was in the precinct coffee room, preparing a jug as Rome walked in.

"Morning, Charlie. How's the wife?" Rome asked.

"Same as always. How was your weekend?"

Rome thought back to sitting with Willa by the lake before skipping to his dream that morning. Her suave smile was the same in both, but one was real, and one was a fantasy.

"Yeah, good, great," he answered, stepping out and over towards his office.

"Oh, did you hear about the storm?" Charlie called out.

"What about it?" Rome paused.

"Apparently, a few shops experienced some hail damage. I thought we should probably check it out," Charlie explained.

Rome sunk, lightly bumping his head on the doorframe. Charlie was right. He should be checking in on the community, especially as the Sheriff... but that also meant he wasn't able to spend time developing leads on the Donohugh case. Which also meant he didn't have an excuse to see Willa.

His mind flashed back to his dream tauntingly, and he snapped his focus back to Charlie.

"Right, let's go."

***

Almost an hour later, Rome and Deputy Charlie were standing at Devonthorpe's council chambers. Once they'd visited a few businesses, Devonthorpe's Mayor Vanessa Hampton invited them to a last-minute meeting. As they waited for the meeting to begin, Rome's phone rang. The caller ID showed it was Joe Mark.

Rome begrudgingly answered. "Sheriff Pendleton speaking."

"Rome, I really think it's time for me to come back now," Joe's voice slithered through.

"Joe, I remember clarifying that it wasn't a suspension," Rome answered.

"Come on, Rome, you know that's unfair."

Rome seethed. "Unfair?"

His mind flickered back to the scene he walked in on that day. Willa had tears in her eyes, and bruises had already formed on her wrists. His heartbeat rose.

"You assaulted an innocent woman, Joe."

"I didn't know she was innocent!"

"So you think it's okay to abuse and act like that either way?"

"I was just trying to get the job done, Rome," Joe answered.

"Nope, wrong answer. You're never coming back to my precinct."

"This is discrimination!" Joe shouted.

"For fucks sake, Joe." Rome hung up the phone and turned back around to Charlie, who was fidgeting in his place.

"So, how'd that go?" Charlie asked awkwardly.

"You don't want to hear it."

The doors in front of them opened, easing the tension.

"You can come in now," Vanessa said, opening the door wide enough for the men to slip through.

Upon entry, Rome nodded in recognition to the other councillors who sat by but saw a woman he wasn't familiar with.

"Sheriff Rome, Deputy Charlie, this is Annabel Hale," Vanessa started.

Rome's eyes widened with recognition.

"Annabel is an environmentalist and climatologist; she's known internationally so we're very lucky to have her here with us!" Vanessa continued.

"Nice to meet you, Annabel," Rome greeted.

"Lovely to meet you both," she smiled while shaking their hands.

"What's brought you here?" Rome asked.

Sure, Willa had told Rome a lot about Annabel already, but he wanted to find some things out for himself.

"She's offered to help us try to organise and redistribute some grants for people who were affected by the storms on the weekend," Vanessa continued.

"I'm aiming to be more involved in the community from here on out," Annabel said.

"Right."

"The grants were also funded by Annabel," Vanessa continued.

"Oh?"

"Well, no need to go sharing that around now, Vanessa," Annabel laughed, appearing humble.

However, after she said so, she looked around the room, making quick and deliberate eye contact with everyone, ensuring they gave her a positive reaction.

Rome tilted his head at the behaviour but remained quiet.

"Well, shall we get started with the meeting?" Vanessa beamed, letting everyone take their seats.

After listening to the council's presentation and observing Annabel, Rome couldn't help but feel a bit irked.

Sure, Annabel was fantastic, but something was off about her. She was too eager to be seen in a particular light, and that made her donations, however impressive, seem insincere. Maybe it was just a point of jealousy or a growing inferiority complex. After all, it appeared he was secretly fighting this woman for Willa's undivided attention. Rome cringed, remembering he appreciated Annabel's presence in Willa's life just the other day.

"Oh, and did you know they nominated Annabel for 'Researcher of the Year'?" Vanessa stated, and Rome tried not to roll his eyes.

Vanessa was making sure she met the boasting standards, and Rome watched Annabel eat it up.

"No, I didn't know that!" Charlie beamed.

Rome shot a daring look at Charlie, earning a confused expression.

"And she's even collaborating with our university's environmental department!" Vanessa continued.

"We know that already," Rome dismissed with passive aggression.

The room turned quiet and looked over to him with confusion, and Rome realised he had spoken aloud. *Yeesh.*

"What Rome means," Charlie began quickly, "is that we're actually well acquainted with Willa Triston, and she's in that department."

"My Willa?" Annabel gasped.

Rome's eyes hardened. "She was selected for your dinner, yes."

"Wow, what a coincidence!" Vanessa said.

"Why is she involved with your precinct?" Annabel asked with a tight smile.

"She's a volunteer investigator," Charlie answered.

"Oh? But you do know she wants to be an environmentalist, right?" Annabel taunted.

"I'm well aware," Rome deadpanned.

Charlie and Vanessa could suddenly place a competitive tension in the room and were unsure how to handle it.

"Well, it's lovely to meet someone so connected with my Willa," Annabel smiled, standing from her seat.

"Likewise," Rome stated, standing as well. His phone buzzed loudly in his pocket, and he stepped to the side.

"Sorry about the interruption. We have to keep them on for emergencies," Charlie apologised on Rome's behalf.

"Sheriff Pendleton speaking," Rome answered from the corner of the room.

"We need units dispatched for a threat at a local university. The suspect is reported to be armed," the emergency services informed.

"Which one?" Rome asked.

"The University of Devonthorpe," they answered, and Rome began to sweat.

"What department?" he prompted.

"Environmental science," they replied.

Willa, he thought.

"I'm on my way," he said, ending the call. "Charlie, we've got an emergency, now!"

Chapter Thirteen

Warning sirens blared throughout the University of Devonthorpe, and lecture halls got bolted shut. It was a campus-wide lockdown, and Willa's heart thumped louder and louder. But how did she end up outside?

It was typical, she thought. Nowadays, she was finding herself in all kinds of tricky situations, and many put her safety in question.

This time, Willa was on her way back from the library when it all began. Professor Hobbs had sent her to photocopy some class notes, since she finished her work early and other students needed extra attention. One of those students was Poppy, so Willa didn't mind too much. Plus, it wasn't unusual for her to be doing these odd jobs.

After the scanner beeped and pieces of paper spat out, Willa gathered them carefully. But as she followed her trail back outside, she noticed a change in atmosphere. There was no one around walking through the outdoor pathways.

She frowned and kept walking onwards, back to her department. As she drew closer, a buzzing alarm surrounded the school, and suddenly the atmosphere made sense. It was a school lockdown.

Willa started running to the lecture hall as her heart rate rose, but to her dismay she could see the doors were shut.

"Damn it," Willa said, running onwards. When she reached the doors, she rattled the handle, but it wouldn't budge.

"Hey! Let me in. It's Willa!" she called out, but there was no answer. As Willa pressed her ear to the door, she heard a muffled noise inside. It was Poppy's frantic voice.

"... She's not... I can't sit... We need to wait..." muffled cries seeped through the seemingly soundproof door.

Willa couldn't make out a lot, but she knew she was the cause of Poppy's dismay. Her friend was both very emotional and very loyal. Knowing Willa was outside and in potential danger, it would've driven her wild.

Willa swung away from the door and sighed. Unfortunately, because of Poppy's episode, Willa's callout wasn't heard. It was a muted effort.

Willa stood back, knowing she shouldn't stay there forever. She didn't know what had caused this lockdown, but she knew it wasn't good. She couldn't continue calling for Professor Hobbs or Poppy without drawing attention to herself.

She ran around the corner, behind an old rectangular statue, and dove her hands into her pockets. If she had a Sheriff on speed dial, she might as well use him.

"Seriously?" she whispered, realising her phone was back at her desk inside.

Bang... Bang... Bang... A strange noise snapped her back into reality, causing her to peek through a crack in the statue. Her eyes zoned in on a metal baseball bat, and she started to shiver. The bat banged back and forth, running across the wall of the lecture hall as the person walked.

Looking away from the bat, Willa's eyes travelled up a strong arm. A man's arm. A man's arm with a tattoo, at that. Feeling giddy about the spot, like a true detective, her eyes narrowed in on the details. It was a tattoo of a pine tree, and though it was small, it was enough to be recognisable. As her eyes continued to travel, she could see the man was wearing a grey t-shirt with black jeans and sneakers.

Reaching his face, she caught her breath. It was like she was watching a horror movie, as a haunted mask covered his face to hide his identity. It was a white mask with a big, black grin and pointed nose.

The mask frightened her more than the bat did as she wondered what he planned to do with a hidden face.

Bang... Bang... Bang... The man walked closer, now only metres away, as he reached the door of the hall. He knew exactly where he was going as if he himself was a student.

Maybe he was? But what did he want?

The man came to a halt and began bashing the blackened glass windows with his bat. They shattered and crumbled in front of him, but they were still barred shut. There was no way he'd fit through with his build. Even Willa would've been too big for it. He was creating chaos to spark fear into those hiding in the lecture hall.

The man kept swinging the bat around, and Willa tried not to flinch each time while maintaining her cover.

"Professor Hobbs! Come out!" he shouted, revealing his target.

Why did he want Professor Hobbs? Was he going to attack him?

After a long moment stuck outside, Willa thought he'd either get bored or give up soon and go away. Plus, even without calling Rome, she was sure that after the alarms went off, he wouldn't be too far away.

As Willa thought of the outcomes, the man threw his bat at the last window, making the glass explode and the bat fall to the ground.

Willa eyed him warily as he bent down to pick it up, finding it strange for him to stay in that position for so long. What was he doing?

Then she realised it. He was looking in her direction. She gazed at her feet and noticed a gap in the statue revealed them. He'd seen her shoes.

"Well, hello there," he spoke.

Willa moved her feet quickly, stepping backward and further into cover – but it was too late. She'd already been seen, and he was creeping over to her position.

In a swift movement, he flung his arm and there was a crash. The man threw the bat in her direction, hitting the glass panelling above where Willa stood.

The glass shattered and sprinkled over her, with light shards sinking into her shoulders.

Willa let out a brief hiss in pain before regathering herself and moving forwards.

This brought her closer to him, but it also meant she was no longer stuck. It was better for her to be in an open area as it allowed more opportunities to escape.

His pace quickened as she began to dash, and she knew she couldn't hold out much longer. Luckily for her, in the nick of time, she heard police sirens. Rome was here.

The man grabbed her elbow mid-stride and swung her into a brick wall. The impact briefly winded her, and she knew she'd feel it the next day. She cried out. "What do you want?"

"None of your business," he yelled back, creeping forward and dragging his picked-up bat along the floor.

"Then why are you hurting me?"

"Just playing my part. Plus, if I can't get to Hobbs, then I might as well have some fun," he said.

Willa heard heavy footsteps, and a familiar voice called out.

"Police! Stand down!" Rome said, and Willa turned to see him holding out his gun. Charlie followed closely behind, and to Willa's confusion, Annabel was right next to him.

The man snickered, holding his bat up once again.

"Stop!" Annabel screeched. He looked between the Sheriff and Annabel, then back to Willa. His hand clutched the bat for a moment, then he released with an exasperated sigh. He stepped back and raised his hands in surrender. Charlie ran forward with cuffs and brought him to the ground, informing him of his rights. Willa finally had the chance to breathe, but her pain began to kick in, too.

"Oh god," Willa said, looking at her blood-stained shirt.

It wasn't enough blood to make her dizzy, but when she hit the wall, some glass shards had pushed in further.

"Willa!" Rome called out. His expression was a mixture of worry and anger, and upon his arrival, he knelt down next to her.

"Rome," she flinched as he reached towards her shoulder.

"Are you okay?" he asked, but he didn't expect an answer. Instead, he looked around at the broken windows, piecing the scene together.

Willa looked up to see Annabel creeping behind them, worry filling her face.

Willa frowned. "Annabel? What are you doing here?"

"Darling, I'm so sorry. Things like this should never happen," she said.

"It's not your fault," Willa brushed off, but Annabel kept going.

"Come with me, I'll clean you up, and you'll be alright."

"I'll be taking her to the hospital," Rome pulled her arm possessively and she winced in response. He looked back feeling guilty, but didn't let go.

She rolled her eyes, following his trail. "Alright, alright, I'll come freely."

As they passed Charlie, Rome nudged him. "Take off his stupid mask and take him to the station," he commanded.

Willa watched the unmasking over her shoulder and noticed the culprit was indeed a student. She'd seen him before, but she didn't quite know who he was.

"Annabel, I'm guessing you can find a way home yourself, seeing as you pushed your way into our car in the first place," he said rudely.

"Rome!" Willa reprimanded his tone.

"It's alright, Willa. You've been through a lot. Let me know when you're out of the hospital," Annabel smiled.

"I promise," she said, walking onwards. Once they were out of sight, Rome dragged her to the nearby tanks. Finally, the sirens of the lockdown stopped blaring, and Willa felt a brewing headache start to settle.

"Why the hell did you treat Annabel like that?" she demanded.

Rome paused, not wanting to berate her idol. However, he knew something was off with Annabel, and if she was who she seemed to be, then Annabel was just pretentious, end of story.

"Look, I'm just worried about you. I'm sorry," he said. It might not have been what he was thinking, but it was still the truth.

She kept her frown, but Rome was just glad she was expressing herself. Willa stayed calm and collected since he'd arrived, but Rome knew that wasn't how she was feeling on the inside. The blood on her shirt deserved at least a couple of complaints, let alone the fact that she went through this at all. Hell, he was in a wreck of a state just from hearing about the emergency.

Rome traced her face with his fingers, letting them trail down to her neck and collar. Willa's breath hitched.

"May I?" he asked, reaching for the buttons of her shirt.

"What are you doing?" she said, pushing his hand away.

"Don't be stupid, Willa. I want to check the wound. Believe it or not, I have some training in first aid," he said, causing her to roll her eyes. "A few of these shards need to come out."

"Right, sure," she sighed. She began undoing her buttons herself to get rid of the awkward tension. Then, after opening a couple, she stretched her collar to the side so that Rome had a clear view of her shoulders, and only that.

"Shit, Willa," he said, frowning.

"Yeah, feels like it," she replied.

He blew lightly on the wounds and held her head in place with the other hand.

"I'll do what I can – but I can't get to the larger ones in case I do more damage."

"Fair enough."

"One moment," he said, spinning around to the tank's spout. He turned it on and brought back a handful of water. "This will sting quite a bit."

He washed the water over her skin, and though it hurt a bit, making Willa wince and grimace, it washed away some smaller glass shards.

He rebuttoned her shirt. "Are you alright?"

"I'm fine," she defended, looking away.

Willa hated feeling vulnerable, and that's precisely what she was today. A lump in her throat surfaced as she tried to hold back tears of shock.

"Willa, it's only me," he said, tilting her chin up. "Say what you need and act how you feel."

Immediately, her eyes began to water, and her lip started to quiver.

"It was terrifying, Rome," she finally admitted.

"Oh dear," his heart broke for her. "Come here."

He pulled her in for a comforting hug, being cautious of his pressure. Surprisingly, she reciprocated, and her left hand grabbed him closer.

"It's alright, you're safe," he whispered.

"You're going to get blood on your shirt," she sniffled into his chest.

He ruffled her hair softly with his hand. "Let's take you to the hospital, alright?"

***

As soon as Willa and Rome arrived at the hospital, Willa was ushered into a room and Rome was left to fill out some paperwork.

It didn't take long for her door to reopen, and though she expected it to be either Rome or the nurse, it was Barry.

"What happened now, Willa?" he asked with concern.

Willa sat for a moment, not knowing what she should say, and realised that she had every right to be honest this time.

"Some vandal attacked the university, and I got caught in the crossfire," she explained, pointing to her shoulder.

"An attack? Oh my god, Willa. Were they arrested?"

"Yeah, he's in custody, I believe," she said, hoping the topic died off.

"Well, that's a relief," he said, still looking worried. "Let's treat this wound."

Willa nodded, unbuttoning her top and taking it off. Unlike around Rome, she wasn't embarrassed. Barry was a doctor.

"This is going to hurt just a bit, but if you can make it through, I have a lollipop for you," he said.

Willa looked at him strangely and let out a soft laugh. "You do realise I'm not that young?"

"I know. I just wanted to lighten your mood," he said, getting some tweezers. "Hold onto my left hand and squeeze it if you feel the need to."

"Right," she said, taking his hand.

When she felt a sharp tugging, Willa winced, and despite what she had thought she would do, she grasped his hand.

"Are you okay?" he asked, pausing.

"Yeah, sorry, just surprised," she said, gesturing for him to go on.

As if pulling out a splinter, he found each piece and extracted it efficiently. He did the same for another two shards, and Willa squeezed his hand each time.

"That seems to be all of it," he said, turning around to grab some gauze.

Willa let go of his hand, and he looked back to reassure her as he continued her treatment. He covered up her wound after putting some ointment on and returned her shirt to her.

"Here you go," he said, giving her a moment to button up.

"Thanks," she said awkwardly, feeling his intense gaze. Fortunately, the ointment relaxed the pain.

"So, how are things going?" he asked, sitting back.

She laughed awkwardly. "Um, yeah, alright, I guess, all things considered."

"I get what you mean, don't worry," he said.

"So, is this all good now?"

"Hmm?"

"My shoulder?"

"Oh, right, yes, that's all fine. You'll just need to come back in a week to get it checked and to make sure it's not getting infected," he said.

"Okay, sounds good. I better find Rome," she said.

"You're with Rome?"

"Yeah, he was at the incident, so he helped and drove me here," she explained the connection.

"Right, well, I guess you better go then," he said.

"Will do," she smiled, standing up from her seat and walking towards the door.

"Willa?" Barry called.

She turned around. "Yes?"

"Would you have dinner with me sometime?" Barry asked.

Willa's jaw dropped slightly, but she picked it up before he noticed.

"Well, I just think we'd enjoy ourselves," Barry continued, sensing her hesitance.

The first thing that came to her mind was, "Is that allowed?"

"You're an adult, and I'm just treating you for a shoulder wound," he said.

Willa snickered, knowing it felt odd... But as she thought, she couldn't deny that she found him attractive. His features were her traditional type.

"Um…" Willa said, feeling unsure.

"How about you let me know next week after you think it over," he asked.

"Next week?"

"At your check-up," he reminded.

"Oh, right, yeah? That sounds like a plan," she said, feeling confused.

"In the meantime, text me, will you?"

She arched a brow. "On what number?"

Barry chuckled and ushered her out of the room. He opened the door with a smooth swing and stood by it. Rome was leaning on the wall directly on the other side of the door, giving him a full view of the situation.

"Oh, good afternoon, Sheriff," Barry said.

"Is she alright?" Rome asked.

Willa gathered her puzzled expression and smiled reassuringly.

"Yeah, I'm fine."

"She's all good. Had a couple painful moments, but it'll get better from here," Barry answered at the same time.

"Thank god," he said, uncrossing his arms and stepping forward to handshake Barry.

"This is the second time I've seen you two together. I didn't know you were that close," Barry said, holding the shake tensely while keeping a smile on his face.

Willa's eyes widened at the body language.

"We're… working together," Rome said, hating his loss for words to describe the situation. Well, it wasn't that he had a loss for words but that he had no other words he was entitled to. Not yet, anyway.

"Ah, I see," Barry grinned, letting go of Rome's hand and then turning to Willa. "I have your number on file, so I meant you should just reply for now."

Rome's posture snapped, and he looked at Willa's response.

"Oh, okay, will do," she coyly responded.

"Well then, I'll be off. You best be as well. See you later, Sheriff, Willa," Barry said, nodding at them both as he walked away.

"Unbelievable…" Rome said, a scowl growing on his face.

"I know right," she paced towards the exit.

Rome fast-walked ahead of her, stopping her in his tracks.

"He's going to text you?" Rome asked.

"Yes…"

"Why?"

"Why can't he?" she challenged.

Rome huffed with a defeated laugh and looked back again. He had answers to that question, but he didn't have the agency to say them. "He said it like you didn't give it to him."

Willa pushed past him, answering as she walked out of the clinic. "He has it on file, just like you did when you tracked me down."

"Oh, don't you turn this on me now," he scoffed, catching up again.

She stopped, turning back to him. "What's your problem?"

"My problem? He's your doctor, Willa. Why is he messaging you?"

"He said he wanted to get dinner," she answered.

Rome choked, realising Barry moved quicker than he thought. "Are you going to go?"

"I don't know yet, Rome. Have you given me a reason not to?"

"But—" he turned quiet. This was his chance to bring up whatever had been going on between them, but he didn't take it.

She rolled her eyes. "Then it has nothing to do with you, alright?"

"You're driving me crazy," he huffed, walking forward to the police car.

He let her in, then entered on his side. When he leant over to buckle the seatbelt, this time, Willa didn't get angry about it. Because of her wound, it wouldn't have been the easiest task to complete herself.

Once she was buckled in, he stayed close, looking right at her eyes.

"What is it?" she asked.

He looked puzzled, not knowing what to say, but eventually leaned back and started the car. They drove all the way to Willa's house before he even spoke a word.

"I'll help you in," he said, getting out of the car and opening the door for her.

"No, it's alright, thanks for taking me to the hospital," she said.

"No worries," apart from Barry, he thought. "Are you sure?"

"You better get back to work, figure out what that guy wanted," she said, trailing back to the investigation.

"I'll figure it out, don't you worry."

"Let me know what happens with it, alright? I know it's not technically my case, but I'm obviously involved."

"I'll talk to you later, I promise."

Chapter Fourteen

Rome marched into the station in a bad mood, slamming the door behind him. But since they were understaffed and Charlie was in the interrogation room, Rome had no one to tell him off for it. Then again, he was the boss, so they wouldn't have a go at him anyway.

He ran a hand through his hair in frustration, moving it along his face as he thought about what he should do.

Now, if it weren't obvious, Rome definitely had feelings for Willa. He couldn't help it – his infatuation took over before he could halt its process.

Heck, maybe he did from the very beginning. But now, was he too late? Just as the two started getting closer, Barry swooped in.

"Fuck off, Barry," he muttered, letting off steam.

As he stood and saw his reflection in the window, Rome knew he was being selfish. He couldn't blame her if they did go to dinner together, and as much as he wanted to, he shouldn't feel entitled to her affections. He had gotten her wrapped up in a world of drama, and she'd been through enough to make her want to take the easy option. Someone simple and put together, like Dr. Barry Whitman.

Plus, he had put her into a work-relationship construct. If he made a move, he'd be breaking the rules, not to mention how uncomfortable she probably would become. So, what could he do?

He gulped, swallowing down his anxiety and finding his resolve. Rome would not sit idly while Willa fell for another man. It wasn't his right, but he knew he worked well with her, and he wouldn't give up. He wouldn't sabotage whatever date they'd go on, but he'd be there for her, and she'd soon be able to choose who she wanted most.

He had two options – say how he felt, or if he was feeling confident, wait for her to make the first move.

Suddenly feeling more motivated than hopeless, he fixed his hair and stood up. Finally, he was in a space where he could focus on the task at hand – getting justice for Willa.

He walked out of his office and knocked on the interrogation room's door.

"We're ready," Charlie called out, and Rome opened the door in response.

Charlie was facing the assailant, arms crossed with his back to the entrance. Rome took a look at the college student and saw him smugly staring back.

"Back for more, old man?" he said with a British accent.

First of all, Rome thought he wasn't old. He was a seasoned youth, a working man, but in no way did that mean he was old.

"Kids with accents shouldn't go around causing trouble in small towns. You're too identifiable," Rome said, ignoring the comment. "Right, Charlie?"

Charlie finally turned around to face him, and for some reason, he was wearing the culprit's mask. Rome's mind flashed back to the night he was attacked – his head wound hurt as he thought back to the first person stepping out from the bushes… unafraid and persistent, despite Rome pulling out his gun. He lost his balance and held the wall to stabilise himself.

Charlie took the mask off and wore a puzzled expression. "Are you okay, boss?"

"Aw, did that scare you?" the perp taunted.

"I swear to god," Rome said, sobering up.

Despite Rome's moment of fear, he also felt like he won the jackpot. They now had a lead – someone in their custody who had to be linked to the electric stint.

Rome swallowed, feeling the back of his recently healed head as he took a seat at the interrogation table. He was now in business mode – and he was ready to make progress.

He glared. "What's your name?"

"Lachlan. Didn't think I'd give that up, did you?" he smirked.

Apparently, he was also stupid.

"Where were you last weekend," Rome inquired, referring to the night of his last shift.

"Huh?"

"Answer him, kid," Charlie said.

"It's none of your business?" he scoffed.

"We can put you away for a whole lot longer if you're not honest now," Rome reminded.

Lachlan looked around before turning back, feeling embarrassed. "I was out."

"Where?"

"With my boyfriend," he said.

"Now, why's that so hard to say?" Charlie asked.

"You'd know why, dickhead."

"Alright now, let's remove the anger. Can he be your alibi for that?" Rome asked, leaning in.

"Yeah... pass me your notepad. I'll write the number down."

Rome passed it over, and Charlie took it once he was done.

"I'll go confirm this, boss," he said, leaving the room.

Rome stared at him for a moment and felt distaste.

"What were you doing at the university today?" he asked.

"I was going to see Professor Hobbs," he huffed.

"Why? And with a baseball bat, at that?"

Lachlan stirred in his seat for a moment, realising Rome wouldn't give in.

"I got paid to," he said.

"Why?" he asked.

"My brother's friend did it, I don't know why," he answered.

"So, he paid you to attack Professor Hobbs?" Rome frowned.

"He said to roughhouse him, and I took the hint."

"Did your brother know about this?"

"No, I don't think so. I don't train with my brother."

"Your brother's friend trains with you?"

"Yeah, we box together."

"What got you into boxing in the beginning? Anger issues?" Rome pressed.

"What's it to you?"

Rome sighed, scratching his head. This kid had some problems, and he was being manipulated to do someone's bidding because of it. Rome hated that, but then again, excuses didn't get him off the hook. He didn't have room for sympathy.

"What's this friend's name, Lachlan?"

"Richard," he said.

"And how old is Richard? and your brother?"

"My brother is 21, but Richard is 32."

Rome frowned… what was a 32-year-old doing, hanging around with these kids? There was a power play involved, and that gave him a sour taste. Better yet, why was he after Hobbs?

"What's your brother's connection with Richard?"

"They used to work together at some logging company until Richard quit for political reasons," he answered, looking bored.

"Political reasons?"

"I don't know, man. I don't know him that well. Something about deforestation," he huffed.

Huh? Rome didn't think he should disregard the odd topic, but he didn't know where it would lead just yet. After all, he was sent to hit off at the head of the environmental science department. It was closer to a motive, but like Lachlan said, he didn't know.

"Why was the money worth it?" he said.

"I want to move out. My family isn't as... accepting," Lachlan answered.

"I see," he said, looking down to the mask on the table. If his alibi checked out, does that mean it's just a popular mask? Surely it's connected? But how? "What's with the mask, Lachlan?"

"Oh, that? It scared you earlier, didn't it?" Lachlan mocked.

"Answer the question," Rome pressed roughly.

"Richard told me to wear it, said it would help me get away with it all... funny how clearly that didn't work, hey?" he laughed.

Rome, however, didn't find it funny. That was another thing that made things look grave for Richard... but it was a link, and he'd take what he could get, no matter how unsettling.

Rome cleared his throat while Charlie came back into the room.

"His alibi checks out," he said, putting the notepad back down on the table.

"Right," he said, not doubting it. Richard was now the next in line for questioning, but as Rome closed his eyes and remembered coming across Lachlan attacking Willa, there was no way they were done yet.

"So, if you were after Hobbs, why did you turn for Willa?"

"Who?"

"What do you mean, who? The girl you attacked," he spat, standing from his seat.

"Oh, easy pickings, I guess," he uttered before seeing Rome's reaction. "Wait, don't get me wrong, I'm not like this... I just got distracted."

"And decided to hurt her?" he asked.

"Look, I think you're missing the point. I'm off my meds and was on a rampage. I've calmed down now, can't you see?"

"That's no excuse," Charlie said disapprovingly.

"Yes, and I'm sorry. Do you want me to say sorry to her? Is that what will help me leave?"

"First of all, don't you dare go near her ever again," Rome warned.

"Oh?" Lachlan said, bemused. "I remember you dragging her away now, a bit attached, are we?"

"Secondly," Rome ignored him, "what makes you think you're leaving?"

"Wait, what?"

"Not only did we catch you red-handed trying to attack a professor, you physically harmed someone who got in the way. Now, you're here, and you're acting like it was a joke. I don't think you should be on our streets," Rome said.

"You can't do this," he said.

"Plus, knowing that you acted like this after a simple bribe, who's to say you won't do it again?"

"You son of a bitch," Lachlan said, spitting on Rome.

"You know that in itself is an offence? Man, you sure are making it easy for me."

Rome stood up, wiped the spit away on his sleeve, and walked to the door.

Before he shut it behind him, he looked back. "Honestly, I feel sorry for your boyfriend. You're a dick."

***

It had been a week since the incident at the university, and Willa was getting impatient. Sure, Rome called that night to let her know about

128

the case moving forward and to give her some reassurance, but nothing since.

She didn't message him first either or call for that matter, but that didn't mean she didn't want him to. Instead, Willa wanted some clarity before she decided.

As she sat in the waiting room of the Devonthorpe clinic, her current problem was whether she was going to agree to go on a date with Barry or not.

"Willa, you're free to go in now," the receptionist called.

Her head snapped up from her magazine, and she made her way his office.

Approaching the doorway, she saw Barry typing away at his desk, with a fitted, slim sweater and a collar peeking over the top.

"Hello," she said, announcing her presence.

His grin took over, and he stood from his chair.

"Well, if it isn't, Willa. Come in."

"You weren't expecting me? I did have an appointment, you know?" she teased.

He laughed. "I know. I've actually been waiting all day for this."

"Oh?"

"Why'd you have to choose a 3pm appointment? That's torturous."

Willa shyly took a seat. "It was the only one available."

"How've you been?" he broke the silence, turning on his professional tone.

"Yeah, I've been good. It's healed well like you thought."

"Can I take a look?" he asked, and she nodded in response.

Now that it wasn't as clinical as she thought, she felt embarrassed and only moved her shirt far enough to expose her shoulder. He brushed his fingers against her collarbone and then stood back with a reassuring smile.

"You're right. You're out of the woods," he said, taking a seat in front of her.

"That's a relief," she said, not knowing what else to say. But she knew it wasn't ending here.

"Now, I want to show you something." He grabbed his phone out of his pocket.

He went into his messages and held it in front of her to see. It was open to their conversation.

She raised a brow. "What about it?"

"If you didn't know, this isn't what I meant by making sure you reply," he said.

She frowned in response. "How come?"

"It's the metaphorical equivalent of having a conversation with a wall, Willa," he joked.

"Oh, whatever," she rolled her eyes with a light-hearted huff.

"It honestly made me nervous, thinking you'd say no to my dinner invitation..."

Well, Willa thought. She hadn't made her mind up yet.

"You wouldn't say no, would you?" his face was doing the equivalent of puppy-dog eyes, and he left little room for her to say no.

She paused for a moment but couldn't find a reason to disagree, despite feeling like she might want to. Why should she? Why not just give it a shot? Who'll even know if it goes sour?

"Of course not," she said, and a wave of relief washed over him.

Yet, she knew that relief was misplaced. Barry was surely aware that any girl would fall for him, and so he wouldn't have doubted his charm. But he wasn't harmful, and it might be some fun in return.

He grabbed her hand and held it as he ushered her out, being on time for his next appointment.

"I can't wait," he said, softly squeezing her palm.

"I guess I'll see you next time," she said, leaving back through the hallway.

As she reached outside, her phone buzzed, and she answered it with a smile.

"Willa, how did it go?" a voice sounded, giving Willa goosebumps.

"Annabel, hi. Yeah, it went well. There was no permanent scarring or tissue damage," she answered.

"Thank goodness, that's such a relief," Annabel exhaled.

"Yeah, I thought so too," she said.

"Anyways, dear. While I have you, I was going to ask if you wanted to come over for dinner tomorrow? Don't worry, I won't burn the food again," she said.

Much to Willa's bewilderment, she had seen Annabel quite frequently. They'd had brunch together twice since the incident, and honestly, it couldn't have come at a better time. Willa needed the distraction.

"Don't be silly, the apple crumble was fine. I don't think anyone can ruin a crumble," Willa laughed.

"I'll take your word for it. Anyway, dinner? Tomorrow?" Annabel went to confirm.

"Actually, I hate to decline, but I have plans tomorrow," Willa answered.

"Oh?"

"Yeah, Poppy and I have an event, and she's been really looking forward to it. How about we take a rain check?" Willa said, walking to her car.

"What event?" Annabel said, not liking being the second choice.

Willa wracked her brain on how to sound scholastic and how to not sound like she was bailing on her mentor for what could be seen as a little too much fun.

"Oh, just some seminar. We had tickets booked already," she lied.

"Of course, but Willa?"

"Yes, Annabel?"

"Don't get into too much trouble. Safety first, remember."

"Yeah, I know. Thank you for checking in," she ended the call.

Annabel was acting like Willa's new parental figure, and honestly, Willa was eating it up.

As she got into her car, her phone buzzed again, but this time it was a text from Poppy.

P: What will you wear tomorrow?

Despite what Willa had told Annabel, they weren't going to a seminar. The Bakery's concert was finally here. Willa didn't care that James was coming anymore even though it meant she'd be third wheeling. As long as she saw the show, she was happy.

But she couldn't reply right away because she didn't know the answer. She'd planned far too late. Instead, Willa thought about the index of her wardrobe the entire drive home.

***

Rome was in his office going through some paperwork until he heard someone at the front door. Charlie was out currently, so Rome knew it was his turn to hold the precinct's front.

As he left his office, he saw a woman with three men in suits behind her, looking more like props than people.

The woman had long, blonde hair, and she wrinkled her nose as she took off some luxury sunglasses.

"How can I help you?" Rome said, getting their attention.

"My name is Penelope Quinn, and I'm actually here on business," she said.

Rome wracked his brain for the name that felt somewhat familiar. He knew of the Quinn Woods, and he also knew about Penelope's involvement with Annabel Hale. He'd done some… investigating, not stalking, when Willa got her first invitation to the golden ticket dinner.

But now that he knew who she was, what business could she possibly have at the precinct?

"Is it a forest licensing issue or something?" Rome asked sincerely, but she chuckled at him rudely in response.

"No, silly," she laughed, turning to one of her lackeys. "Nick, won't you show him?"

The man to her left walked forward and took a piece of paper from his suit's inner breast pocket. "We have a release order from the State Department for Lachlan, with all charges dropped."

"Wait, what?" Rome frowned, taking the piece of paper to see for himself.

"It's legitimate. See the stamp in the corner?" Nick pointed. Like he said, there was indeed the Police Minister's signature stamp.

"On what terms? Why?" Rome asked, bewildered.

"That's a need-to-know basis," Penelope chirped, butting in once more. "So, go on, how long is this going to take?"

"Do you even know what he's done?" Rome frowned.

"Small, tedious details," Penelope said.

"Lachlan attacked a student at his school," he frowned, and Penelope's eyes trailed down Rome's body as he spoke, landing on his waist.

"It was a mistake, and the minister recognises it. You can't keep him here any longer," she said as she reached out for the keys that dangled on his belt. Rome stepped away, deflecting her hand in the process.

"Don't." His eyes showed a notion of fierceness, and a smirk spread across on Penelope's face as he finally gave in. "I'll get him."

Rome angrily walked to the holding cell where he had kept Lachlan, knocked on the door, and got his attention.

"What do you want? Here to tell me another shitty joke?" He rolled his eyes.

Rome cleared his throat and hoped that Penelope and her escorts hadn't heard. "No, you're being let out. Stand up, and I'll open up."

"What? Are you serious?" Lachlan asked, snapping to attention.

Rome opened the door, released his cuffs, and slapped a hand on Lachlan's shoulder to escort him out.

They returned to the precinct entrance where Penelope waited, but Rome squeezed Lachlan's shoulder and whispered in his ear.

"You do anything more to Willa or that school, and you'll wish I never knew you," he threatened.

"Whatever," Lachlan grumbled, but he was wise enough to recognise the intensity of Rome's threat.

Penelope looked over to Lachlan at that moment, while Rome waited silently at the end of the walkway.

"Oh, darling! How'd they treat you? Are you alright?"

"Um… Yeah, I'm fine," Lachlan said, looking back over. "Do you know me?"

"I've heard great things about you," she smiled, taking his arm and peering back to Rome. "Thanks for your cooperation," she mocked.

Penelope's lackeys nodded at Rome and then followed her outside. Rome thudded his head against the wall and huffed as he picked up his phone. However, he heard the doorbell ding again, and the person he was going to call entered the room.

He sighed. "Charlie, Lachlan's gone."

"Gone?" Charlie's eyes snapped wide open, and he reached for the gun in his holster. "Which direction?"

"No, no. He didn't escape," Rome huffed, sitting on the office counter. He grabbed the release form and waved it at Charlie. "Penelope Quinn came earlier with an order for his release."

Charlie gaped. "You're joking."

"Read it yourself," he said, passing it over.

"And this was approved by the State Department?"

"I couldn't believe it either."

Charlie took a moment to think and locked eyes with Rome once more. "Wasn't Penelope that forest chick?"

"If you mean she made the Quinn Woods, then yes," Rome answered, looking puzzled.

"Didn't Lachlan say that... wait, who was his brother's friend?"

"Richard," Rome prompted impatiently.

"Didn't Lachlan say that Richard was big on being against deforestation?" he asked.

Rome considered the idea, and his eyes widened.

"Shit, Charlie. I think we have ourselves a conspiracy."

Chapter Fifteen

Willa was sitting at home scrolling through her phone while she waited for the day to pass and the concert to arrive. There were three hours before she had to leave, and in Rome's radio silence, all she had was Barry to keep her entertained.

As she looked over their texts, she frowned. She knew Barry told her to change her message style, but she had nothing better to work with. Maybe it was because they had little to talk about? After all, they didn't really know each other. Maybe it was because they had no chemistry? Or perhaps it was because Willa wasn't actually interested... but their conversations were, for the lack of a better word, boring.

She put her phone down and looked at her outfit in her lounge room mirror. Willa was already dressed for the concert and felt somewhat proud of herself for being productive. She sported a green and white gingham dress with spaghetti straps and a t-shirt styled underneath.

She stood up and twirled on her toes to her reflection, watching her '70s style curled hair flounce around her until she heard the doorbell.

"That's weird," she said aloud, remembering she was going to meet Poppy at the concert.

She flung her door open regardless with an excited grin but was then startled by the unexpected guest.

"Hey, Willa."

Her forehead creased with confusion. "Rome..."

"How's your shoulder?" he held his breath.

Willa moved it around fluidly as if to give him an answer but then stopped and frowned. "You're a bit late to ask that," she said.

"I know, I'm so sorry, things got hectic at the station," he answered, feeling gutted. "The case had a new angle, so I had to take care of that first before I let you know what was going on."

"Right." Willa knew things were out of his control and that her feelings might be a bit immature, but she still felt she deserved to act this way.

"Is it alright if I come in?" he asked.

"Sure," she stood to the side, allowing him to enter.

She wasn't mad at him, and it's not like he didn't answer her calls or anything. She'd only just gotten used to him spamming her with messages, so she felt somewhat lonely.

Rome took in her appearance and then locked eyes with her. "You look lovely."

Willa smiled a little. "Thank you."

Rome froze up, letting out more words. "Is it for your date?"

"No, it's for a concert," she answered.

"Oh? What one?"

"Ever heard of The Bakery?"

"Willa, just how old do you think I am?" he chuckled, sitting on the couch.

"Rome?" she sat down next to him.

"Yeah?"

"I missed you," she answered, without looking in his direction.

However, Rome didn't worry about looking desperate. Instead, those words pulled his attention right in, and he eyed her side profile with intensity. "I missed you too."

"So," she shifted the mood and turned his way. "What happened this week?"

"Actually, we found a lead."

"What? Really?" she grinned.

"It turns out the person who... attacked the school," he said, not knowing how to put it lightly, "he was paid to do it. To hurt Professor Hobbs."

"Oh?"

"There are still some strange loose ends that need to be determined, but the person who hired them to attack the school, they are the same group of people who attacked me too while we were doing our watch," he said.

"Wow," she exhaled, feeling anxious that they'd shared a similarly poor experience. "So, what are the loose ends?"

"Another link between the two groups, but nothing is confirmed yet," he said, knowing that attacking one of her idols wouldn't be a good idea.

Unfortunately, Willa had a way of getting things out of him.

"What link?"

"Charlie and I think Penelope Quinn is involved," he said.

"What?"

"The school intruder's name is Lachlan. He was actually hired by a man named Richard, who used to work with his brother. They stopped being friends after Richard quit his job because of political reasons," he said.

"What do you mean?"

"He was a tree logger and then became an advocate for anti-deforestation," Rome explained.

She wasn't convinced. "Right, that would do it... so you think because of that detail, Penelope is involved?"

"Penelope was the person who bailed him out yesterday," he said.

"Wait, he's out?" Willa asked, feeling goosebumps travel along her skin.

Rome noticed her change in comfort and reached for her hand, holding it reassuringly.

"Let's just say he's sobered up. You're safe, Willa," he said.

"Why was Penelope able to let him out?"

"I wasn't told. Apparently, even though I'm the local Sheriff dealing with the matter, I don't have the right to know. So, she organised it with my superiors," he said.

"So, if Penelope is sketchy, then do you think your bosses are too?" she was catching up quick.

"I'm not saying anything. I called them loose ends for a reason," he answered.

"Right."

"So, what do you think?"

"Honestly, it's a lot to be just a coincidence, I get that…" Willa thought back to meeting Penelope at Annabel's dinner. "Then again, anything more is a bit of a stretch, don't you think?"

Rome watched Willa become reserved and knew precisely why. He wasn't going to judge her for being loyal to Annabel and her crew, but this couldn't get out of hand. If he was right, Rome just hoped she'd see reality for what it was. After all, she was pretty much all he and Charlie had – especially if his higher-ups weren't to be trusted.

"Yeah, it probably is a stretch," he said. But for the first time since they both met, he was lying.

Willa looked at the clock and realised that time had raced by.

"Well, it's about time that I call a cab," she said.

"Do you want me to drive you?" he offered.

She laughed. "No, it's alright. I don't think I'll have many friends if I rock up in a cop car."

"Are you planning on hanging out with fugitives?" he jokingly warned as they walked out.

"I guess you'll see if I get caught," she laughed in response, locking the door behind her.

"Don't joke about that," he said, stopping in her way. She looked up at him, tilting her head at the severe sudden tone.

"You've had all week to make an effort, but you left me on my own. So why care now?"

"Willa, I'm honestly sorry about that," he said.

"Why do you care, Rome? Why are you here now?"

"Don't you know?"

She pushed past him. "Apparently not."

"I don't know what's happening now," he said, trailing behind her. "I thought we were doing okay?"

"I don't have the time for this, Rome."

"Is it because of Barry? You don't want to get close to me because of him?" He stopped in his place, reaching out for her hand to stop her mid-stride.

She turned around. "Clearly, you don't know either," she sighed, stepping into the elevator.

"What?" he asked. Willa sighed and shut the door.

Once the elevator reached the lobby, Willa rushed out and got into the cab waiting down below.

The concert grounds were 20 minutes away, and so Willa took a moment to think about what she wanted and what she just did. She was usually a calm person, but lately she was having more tantrums than she'd like to admit. She looked at her phone, opened Barry's contact, and typed out a message to ease her frustration.

***

When she finally arrived, Willa paid the driver and stepped out of the car. Then, she walked over to her and Poppy's designated meeting spot – the drinks tent outside.

140

It was officially the weekend, so Willa was ready to let loose for the first time in a long while.

"Poppy!" she approached her blonde friend, who was decked out in a pink skirt and crop top combo, paired with some fun cowboy boots.

Now, Poppy was by no means a cowgirl, but these vintage boots of hers were like a lucky charm, and she'd wear them at any outdoor event to keep sturdy.

"Willa, you made it!" Poppy squealed on her approach, barging past James.

"How much time until they go on? Because I could use a drink," she said, eyeing her beverage.

"No worries, James has you sorted," she said, pointing at the two cups he was holding.

"How are you doing, Willa?" he smiled on approach, passing her a drink that appeared to be apple cider.

"A lot better now. Are you excited?"

"James is just here for the company, apparently," Poppy rolled her eyes.

"Hey, I'm always down for a night of fun! But she's right. I think I only know two songs?"

"And you didn't think of studying up earlier?" Willa teased.

He laughed. "Poppy said the exact same thing."

"Also, what do you mean by you're a lot better now?" Poppy asked quietly, ushering her away to give them some space. "What happened?"

Willa didn't like being an open person, but she felt Poppy might know how to help. So she took a big gulp of her cider and let out two words she never thought she'd say. "Boy troubles."

"*What?*" Poppy's eyes widened with excitement.

"So, my doctor asked me on a date?" she started.

Poppy frowned. "Is that even allowed?"

"I guess we're both consenting adults."

"But what happened with Rome?"

Willa grimaced. "A lot, and nothing at all, it's tough to tell with our workload. He wasn't pleased about Dr. Barry, though."

Poppy grinned again. "I always knew there was something there."

"I really like Rome," she sighed. "But we've built something good, and I really don't know how things will turn if I try to make a move. What if it goes wrong?"

"I think you're overthinking it, but I can see where you're coming from. I mean, you don't actually work for him; you can do as you please, right?"

"Yeah, you're right there. We do blur a lot of lines anyway," she said, trying to cover up that last point. She chugged the rest of her drink and looked out to the front. "Hey, I think the support act is starting."

The openers were a small band with only two people on stage, one with a microphone and one with a soundboard. Willa had no clue what their band name was but thought it'd still be nice to head down and listen to them.

"James, let's head in!" Poppy said.

***

Rome trudged into his own house for what seemed like the first time in a while. Since things had gotten heavier over the past week, Rome was sleeping at the office. He had even packed a suitcase with everything he'd need to stay there for as long as it took, but the longer he stayed there, the less he found he was getting anywhere.

Sure, he now had a suspect linked to Penelope Quinn, linked to the cable issues, and linked to his attacker, but he still knew he had to go further. Why didn't the police force have his back? Why did they make him stay quiet about the accidents in nearby towns? Nothing made sense to him, but it all stank of corruption.

And if they were corrupt, who was Penelope Quinn really? And who was Annabel Hale?

He slumped on his bed, stretching out his legs in exhaustion. Whoever they were, he didn't like how close they were to Willa… Annabel's fixation bothered him before any of this new information came to light.

His phone buzzed, and he reached to answer it, taking note that there was no caller ID.

"I hate private numbers," he mumbled, accepting the call. "Pendleton speaking."

"Hey Rome," the voice was eerily familiar.

"Joe… What do you want?" Rome propped himself up into a seated position.

"I just want you to know that I've been thinking about everything, and I know where I went wrong," he said.

Rome rolled his eyes, ready for another attempt for him to beg for his job back. "And where would that be, Joe? Before or after you assaulted a girl?"

"Before then, before it all," Joe's voice sounded gritty. "I went wrong when I started listening to you."

"Oh?" Rome felt almost amused.

"You never respected me or my abilities," he said.

"What abilities, Joe?" Rome mocked.

"Even now! You're taking the piss out of me, but you know what? I know what it's like to have power again," he started.

Rome could sense something was going on, and his ears pricked up. "Go on…"

"We're taking back the city, and we're starting with the stadium," he said.

"What stadium, Joe?" Rome asked. He had little faith in Joe, but Willa was at a stadium at this very moment, and that was his first priority.

"The Macgregor, be here in an hour, or you'll regret it."

Rome relaxed the slightest bit, knowing that The Bakery was playing on the Riverside Stage and that Willa was safe from... whatever mischief Joe was up to. But was this fool really putting others in danger?

"What do you plan to do?" Rome got up, grabbing his keys and putting on a voice record function on his phone call.

"You'll see, it'll teach you for underestimating me!"

"Joe, wait—" Rome started, but Joe ended the call abruptly.

Rome had to think. There was a chance that this was all a bluff for attention since Joe was unstable... but as the Sheriff of Devonthorpe, he couldn't have something go wrong on his watch.

Rome immediately dialled Charlie's work number.

"Charlie, I need you to come to The Macgregor with me right now. Joe's threatening to do something."

"Joe? Joe Mark?"

"The one and only, could you call for backup?"

"Yeah, absolutely. Do you know what type of threat?" Charlie asked.

"No, but he implied it was dangerous. Is anything on at The Macgregor tonight?"

"No sports that I know of," Charlie responded.

"Then why the appeal..." He let his mind wander back to the electricians.

"He said he finally had power... you don't think he meant literally, do you?" Rome asked, heading out his door and hurrying to his police car.

"I guess we'll know when we get there," Charlie sighed.

Rome put on his sirens and raced to the stadium that was only 20 minutes from his home. While Joe said to get there in an hour, Rome thought that maybe he could stop something before it started, whatever it was that he had in mind.

"Fucking Joe," Rome blurted in frustration as he raced through the streets.

Once he reached the stadium, he saw Charlie's car already parked inconspicuously nearby. Rome chose to park beside it, hiding the bulging police car from the main public view. He jumped out and met his deputy in person.

"Sheriff, you ready?" Charlie asked.

"Yeah, I'll go in first, then let you know when to follow behind me." Rome drew the gun from his holster and entered the eerie entrance of The Macgregor. The empty stadium was as off-putting as a nightclub in the daylight. You could see every spilt drink on the floor, gum that would stick to your shoes, and worst of all, an echo that would follow you around.

While he noticed these factors, Rome couldn't see a nearby threat, so he nodded for Charlie to follow behind him. "Let's move."

Rome tiptoed around the stadium for a while and decided it was emptier than he expected – with no Joe insight.

"Let's find some lights," Rome called out.

Charlie flicked a switch he found near the entrance. When the lights came on and he looked around, he guessed they were on edge for no reason. "Do you think we're just too early?"

Rome thought for a minute about the possibility, but he doubted the time really mattered to Joe that much. He checked his watch, and it was the 59-minute mark.

"I guess we wait it out then," Rome said, on full alert with eyes on the entrance.

The time on his watch kept ticking until he heard a ping on his phone – a message notification from an unknown number.

U: Fooled you, Sheriff.

"It was a set-up," Rome said, feeling pissed off. "Charlie, call off the backup."

"Sure thing." Charlie said, leaving the main stadium ground to make his call.

At that moment, Rome's phone pinged with another anonymous message. However, this time, it was a photo — a photo of a mask the attackers were using.

Rome gasped as his new-found suspicions were confirmed. Joe was one of them.

Chapter Sixteen

W illa was drunker than she thought after volunteering to make back-and-forth trips to the in-house bar. She was currently holding two rum and cokes and her own apple cider as she beelined back to where Poppy and James were dancing.

The opening act was now over, and they were grooving to the music playing between the sets.

She caught James' eye as she approached, and he came forward to help free her hands.

"Thanks, Willa!" Poppy called out over the loud music. Soon after, a countdown started, and smoke machines decorated the stage.

"Holy frick, it's them," Willa's eyes opened wide in awe.

Even James cheered with the crowd as the lead singer approached the microphone. As expected, their opening song was their most famous.

"This is one that I actually know," James joked, singing along to the lyrics.

Like with most mosh pits, a wave of people tried to get a closer spot, pushing Poppy, James, and Willa around and into the people in front of them.

"Sorry!" Willa called out, trying to regain her footing. She noticed cable wires beneath her and blamed them for her near fall.

Willa sipped her drink and continued to dance, but her eyes turned a bit hazy from the impact. She was more of a lightweight than she thought.

"You right?" James asked them both as the crowd settled.

After the push, Poppy was now standing behind two men almost twice her size, and she couldn't see a thing. Willa saw a gap forming to her left and got Poppy's attention. "Over there!"

"I'm just going to go in a bit closer if that's okay!" Poppy called out to James behind her, following Willa's direction.

With Poppy gone, Willa was now stuck with James. "So, the tagalongs get stuck without the mega fan," he chuckled.

Willa grinned. "Oh well, we'll have a good time anyway."

The pair listened to the band until the next song finished and James spoke up. "Willa, can I tell you a secret?"

"Um, it depends?" she questioned. Hopefully he knew she was loyal to Poppy if it was anything bad.

"It's good, don't worry. Well, I think so," James laughed, sensing her hesitation.

She smiled. "Fire away then."

"I'm thinking of proposing to Poppy soon," he spoke out.

"*What?*" she shouted, feeling stunned.

"I mean, we've been together since forever, and I know we're young, but I couldn't see myself without her by my side," he blushed.

Willa grinned at how mushy James could be. This was a side she didn't usually get to see from him, but it was refreshing to know how much he truly loved her friend.

"James, this is incredible news," she encouraged him.

"Really? Thank god, I thought people might think I was out of my depth."

"You just said you've been together forever. I'm sure if she thought that, Poppy would've mentioned it by now," Willa joked.

He laughed. "That's a good point, actually."

"So, how are you going to do it?" she shouted as the music ramped up in volume.

"I was thinking of asking her tonight, but I want it to be more romantic than a sweaty concert. I'm a man of class, after all," he smirked.

"Oh, sure you are. Righto," Willa snickered. "I'm so excited for you both though, I don't have a doubt in my mind about her feelings for you."

James gave out a genuine smile. "Thanks, Willa. It means a lot to hear you say that."

They phased their focus back onto The Bakery, and before they realised, the crowd had moved once again, giving them all a gap next to Poppy.

"Shall we head in?" Willa asked and James replied with a curt nod.

As they made their way through, Willa thought about how helpful James' tall stature was when following in crowds. Poppy won't have an issue locating him for the rest of her life.

Rome is tall too, she thought, immediately feeling embarrassed.

She kept walking behind James, feeling distracted, and found her feet almost trip again.

Damn cables, she thought. She must've been drunk if she couldn't deal with a bit of foot traffic.

But as the crowd got thicker, and the air felt thinner, Willa wasn't just feeling drunk – she was now feeling faint, too.

She called out ahead of her. "Hey, James?"

"Yeah?"

"Can you make it to Poppy alone? I think I need to leave the pit. I'm feeling a bit ill," she said.

He turned around, looking over at her. "You okay? Need me to come with you? Poppy will understand."

She smiled, trying to reassure him. "No, that's too much. I'm alright."

"Whatever you say, call us if anything changes!" he said.

"Will do!" Willa responded, turning around and weaving through the sea of people, waving their hands in the air.

Her eyes felt hazy while she passed an alleyway, noticing the people in it were wearing something strange... but she didn't have time to care. She needed a seat.

She found a little spot at the top of the hill looking over the stage. While she was further away, the projector gave her a perfect view.

It took a whole song for her to feel better before she took out her phone. It had two missed calls from Rome, but she begrudgingly ignored them. So now he thinks he can be needy? *Not today, pal.* Instead, she finds her group chat with Poppy and James.

W: I'm just to the left of the food tent, in direct line of the stage.

Shortly after, James replied with a thumbs up. Getting out of that message, she looked over what she sent to Barry in the cab.

W: Hey Barry, I'm sorry, but I don't think I can go on a date after all. I hope you understand. Thanks for everything.

Willa winced at the lack of response. Was she delicate enough? There wasn't a single emoji, so perhaps not. Though she knew she shouldn't expect an answer quickly anyway – Barry was a busy man. But after seeing Rome that afternoon, despite how bad it went, Willa knew who her feelings leapt to... and as she thought, it wasn't Barry.

"Damn you, Rome," she said as she stared at the two missed calls. He knew where she was tonight, so she thought he would be tactful and not bother her until the concert ended.

She felt energised by her misplaced rage and deleted the missed calls, continuing to listen to the boys upfront.

"We're almost done here, but it's been a blast, Devonthorpe!" the guitarist shouted. "You can expect us to come back with another tour soon, but in the meantime, we only have one more song!"

Everyone in the crowd screamed, and Willa cheered along at the new tour announcement. But suddenly, something didn't feel right. She looked to her side at the concert's food trucks – there was a smell drifting through the air, one that felt familiar. The more she sniffed, the fouler it smelt. "What on earth…?"

She heard another scream coming from the main stage. This time, instead of cheers, even in her drunken state, Willa knew it was one filled with terror. A rush of people headed up the hill in her direction, and Willa snapped up from her seat.

It was a swarm… a stampede, and she didn't know why. But she knew something had to be wrong as she saw the band being escorted off the stage by security. Willa reached for her phone amidst the crowd's hustle and called Rome.

"Willa, hey," he answered.

"Rome, something's wrong," she shouted over the noise.

"What's going on over there?" he asked. She wondered if he could hear the screams in the background.

"I'm not sure, but you might want to come down…" she began fading her sentence away as she climbed back down the hill to get a better view.

"Right, I'm on my way, but Willa, get out of there!" he said.

Feeling scared, she said, "Poppy and James are down there."

"Willa—" Rome started warning, but she gathered her courage and hung up. She navigated through the oncoming crowd, getting bumped left and right.

"Run!" a man shouted at her as he pushed past, leaving her heart racing.

As she neared the front of the stage, the smell changed once again, and it was now burnt, rotten odour.

"Poppy! James!" Willa called out, looking around. As she turned, she saw paramedics swarm in, following her against the rush. She kept her eye on a medic as she brushed past, seeing the woman kneel to the ground.

When Willa saw why she knelt, Willa had the urge to vomit. Someone in a glittery leotard was lying lifeless on the grass. Their skin looked fried, and at that moment, Willa linked the smell that she'd been familiar with all this time… the smell of burnt human bodies.

Tears of panic began streaming from her eyes as she continued on with her mission. "Poppy! James!"

She arrived at the left-hand side of the stage, where she and James last saw Poppy before she left the crowd. Her heart rate picked up as she scanned the area, trying desperately to recognise her friends.

With so many fleeing, it didn't take long for the area to clear, and for a signature pink outfit to catch her eye.

It was Poppy, and she was lying on the floor next to James.

Willa wiped her eyes and found the courage to step forward, hoping in every step that they were okay.

But unfortunately, as she came closer, the similar, distinctive smell became stronger.

"Poppy!" she cried out, kneeling at her side.

Poppy's burns weren't severe, unlike the previous person she saw on the ground – but when Willa tried to shake her awake, she wouldn't come to.

Willa searched for vital signs, quickly reaching out a shaky hand to check her pulse. *Thump, thump, thump.* Poppy was alive.

"I need help!" she called out to the nearby paramedics, feeling the slightest bit relieved.

As she saw someone approach, she hurried over to check James, who was groaning beside Poppy. He wasn't burnt, but he'd clearly been trampled by the crowd. Willa knelt to the ground beside them, crying out in fear of what might happen next.

***

After Willa's urgent call, Rome was already in his car speeding over to the Riverside Stage. He had Charlie prepped to meet him at the scene as fast as he could.

Rome heard ambulance sirens in Willa's phone call, and whatever happened, he knew it had to be more than the school threat. That left him in a nervous wreck. Maybe it was because Willa was there, but this muted response felt familiar. Why were medics alerted before him? He couldn't help but think of the accident on the outskirts of town.

And if it was the same thing, then not only was Willa in danger; it also proved his department's corruption. But then came his next worry, was Joe's prank from earlier that night really over? Almost right on time, Charlie's voice came through the car's radio.

"Rome, do you think the prank was a distraction?" Charlie's concern seeped through his voice.

Rome sighed, knowing it was true. After all, Joe had a mean streak, and a silly prank didn't seem like the end of things.

If you thought about it logically, both stadiums were on opposite sides of Devonthorpe. If Joe wanted to distract Rome and Charlie from something at the Riverside Stage, sending them running to The Macgregor was the perfect misdirection.

Rome gritted his teeth and cursed, speeding up further. He was played, and he felt he should've known better... and if Willa got caught in the crossfire because of it, he didn't know what he'd do.

***

Willa had followed alongside Poppy and James as they were taken to the side stage exit. But due to the different types of injuries, the couple had to separate, and Willa couldn't even pick a side.

"No passengers, we don't have space," a medic said.

It made sense. After all, so many patients needed to stack inside the vehicles, and Poppy was still unconscious. It meant nothing for Willa to be by her side, apart from Willa's own personal reassurance.

As she stood watching Poppy's ambulance depart, she was now stone-cold sober and cursed herself for being the only one okay.

But she still didn't understand... What on earth happened?

As Willa walked onwards, both hands drying her eyes, she tripped on a cord. The same cable she tripped on earlier that evening.

Willa stood in her place as her eyes followed the cord's trail, and she saw bodies decorating its path. In her new sober state, she finally remembered where she had seen these cords before. They were what the electricians were dealing with underground, and now they were exposed.

Poppy had been electrocuted, as well as nearly a hundred innocent people in its wake.

Willa's heart froze as she recalled another memory from when she left the stage. The alleyway.

Willa ran in the direction of the alleyway she saw earlier, where she felt something was up. And like she thought as she peered around the corner, they were still there.

These people weren't wearing festival masks, but ones that she had seen before. If only she'd focused earlier, she would've known what was going on. It was the same mask that Lachlan wore when he attacked her... the same one that Rome said people wore when he was attacked guarding the electrical sites.

"This is what they were doing," she realised with a shaky voice.

Willa knew that the electrical hijacking was taking place this whole time, but they didn't know what it meant for them once they got their way. With death on her conscience now, Willa didn't know what to do. It was all because they couldn't solve the case fast enough.

With so much new information rumbling around in her head, she forgot she was still in danger. She peered into the alleyway once more and saw two men in masks clinking their beers together. *They were celebrating.*

Due to the sight of them, mixed with the putrid smell of burned flesh, Willa once again felt the urge to throw up, and her nerves couldn't stop it.

She leaned over out of view to throw up in the bushes, and then returned to her spot as quickly as she could. But this time, her place had been compromised. The two men in masks were now looking directly at Willa, and one climbed the fence behind them to flee.

"Stop!" she shouted, turning around to call for help.

But she was too late, no one was around to help, and the medics were busy attending victims of the crime.

When she waved her head around once more, bravely stepping forward, the second masked bandit started climbing the tall fence as well, forcing her to pick up her pace.

Willa didn't know what she'd do if she got to them. They were *murderers*, after all. But despite it being an uneven fight, she knew had to charge on.

She reached the fence in time to grab the leg of the second masked climber, trying to pull at it as hard as she could.

He struggled, kicking around at her, hoping for her to let go. "Get off me, you stupid bitch!" he called out, and the voice sent chills through her body.

The shock made her let go, giving him the chance to climb away.

"You remember me, don't you?" the man mocked from the other side of the fence while reaching for his mask.

He took it off and let it drop to the floor as his cold, hardened eyes met Willa's own.

"Joe."

Chapter Seventeen

Within seconds, Joe had raced around the corner out of sight with his fellow henchmen, and Willa finally had a second to process what happened.

She ran to the gutter by the wall and started throwing up again. After lurching out more than what she thought was in her stomach, she trudged out of the alleyway and looked over the field once more.

"Oh my god…" she uttered.

Tears streamed down Willa's eyes at the sight, and she felt hopeless. The paramedics were far too understaffed to deal with the catastrophe at hand. When she heard police sirens approaching the area, she knew it was time to brief Rome on what happened.

Willa gathered the courage to walk back onto the field. Her instincts told her to stay away from anything that resembled an electrical cable.

Looking back and forth, she finally saw Rome and Charlie coming through the front gate. He looked as shocked as she did at the situation… but there was something more in his eyes. It was almost a sense of familiarity. Rome was piecing it together.

She ran until she was in his line of sight, already relieved by his presence.

"Willa!" he called out, rushing her way.

Seeing her physically safe gave Rome some peace of mind, but he knew she was distraught. As soon as he reached her, her legs let go, and he caught her weight in an upright embrace.

"It was Joe… he was here, I just tried to chase him, but he got away!" Willa cried out.

"Wait, what?" he stood back, looking her in the eyes. "I had a bad feeling… but you chased him?"

"I couldn't just let them get away after everything! I saw the people in masks while I was up on the hill… if I was still down with Poppy and James… people are dead, Rome!"

"I'm so sorry, Willa…" he took a moment to see from her perspective. What happened, happened, and she didn't need to be chastised. "We'll find a way to catch them, I promise. What did you see?"

Rome hated that he had to interrogate her now, but while he wanted to support her, he had to focus on the case. From what he could tell, countless people seem to be either injured or deceased, and that took priority.

"I was up on the hill because I felt a bit fuzzy, and I saw them. They were wearing masks, but I didn't catch on until it was too late. I couldn't see clearly. Shit, Rome, could I have stopped this?"

Rome's eyes widened as he grabbed her face. "No, no, don't you dare think that! You're lucky to be alive, don't blame yourself!"

Her head sunk, and he knew that wasn't enough reassurance for her right now. She was a smart girl, and with that comes a lot of self-reflection. But he didn't think it was her fault at all – she's one girl against a group of dangerous people, now mass murderers. How could she even stop them if she tried? But thinking about her guilty conscience, he could understand where she was coming from. What she needed was a distraction, and he didn't have time to console her just yet.

"Are your friends okay? Where are they now?"

"They're at the hospital. I should go, shouldn't I?"

He wrapped his arms around her once again, nuzzling his head into her hair before pulling away and agreeing. "I'll get to work. I'll talk to you later."

"Right," she said, freeing herself and walking away. Everyone was already being evacuated, so she followed the line out the gates.

Rome looked around to see the situation for himself. Now that he knew Willa was safe, he had a clear view of what was going on.

He ran over to Charlie, who was talking to the Chief Medical Officer on the scene. As Rome approached, Charlie told the woman he'd brief Rome in so that she could get back to work too. She moved on, heading the other direction just as Rome arrived.

"It's not good, there were over sixty pronounced dead on the field, and many more in a critical condition needing emergency care," Charlie sighed, looking out at the scene.

"Joe was here," Rome gritted his teeth.

"Wait, are you sure?" Charlie was aghast.

"Willa saw him. He has a grudge against us at the precinct, and now it seems he's continuing his misplaced vendetta towards her too... he knew she'd be here," Rome spat with rage.

"That bastard," Charlie said, lifting his hands to his head. "Sixty lives are lost because of him!"

"It's not just him... he was here with the other masked culprits – he's now a part of their crew."

"You're kidding... so this was their plan? Everything was leading up to a horrific slaughter?"

"We still don't know why, but Charlie, this doesn't feel right. It's the same as the incident weeks ago before it was all silenced."

Charlie was shocked. "Are you saying we should withhold information on the case if we're asked?"

"Just in case... with an event like this, you and me? We're on our own now."

Charlie frowned, knowing this was their only option. "Alright."

***

A dark sky spilled over the day's nightmare, and Willa had been sitting in the hospital waiting room. Poppy's parents were currently checking in on her, and only a few visitors were allowed inside at a time.

Willa had only met her parents, Leonard and Rachel, once or twice, but they were very attentive to their daughter. They lived on the same street, they paid her tuition and embraced James as part of their family.

The thought of Poppy and James made Willa's throat jam up.

The waiting room doors opened, and out came the parents.

"How is she?" Willa stood up immediately.

Rachel was in a weak state, crying feebly by her husband's side. Because of this, Leonard realised he had to stay strong and do the talking.

"The doctor said she's stable, thank god, but she's still passed out now. A mix of both the alcohol and the shock," he said.

"I'm so, so sorry... to you both," Willa's lip quivered offering her apology.

"For what? Sweetheart, you didn't do this!" Rachel suddenly adopted mum mode, holding her arms out to hug Willa.

"She's right; we know she's the party animal, not you. Plus, what happened today was dreadful. That poor boy is in much worse condition... and when Poppy finds out..." Leonard's strength faded, and he sobbed alongside them.

"Would you like to go in now?" Rachel changed the topic. "She may be asleep, but it might give you some peace of mind like it did for us. We'll go back in after we get something from the canteen."

"Yes, I would love to," Willa stood up, avoiding her own puffy-eyed reflection in the door windows. She said goodbye to Leonard and Rachel before following through the small hallway to where Poppy was being monitored.

160

There she was, sleeping soundly. Her perfect blonde hair was messed just a little, and her hospital gown hid any evidence of her trauma.

Willa sat beside the bed, careful not to wake Poppy up. To recover, her body would need all the rest she could get.

"I'm so sorry, Poppy…"

Though she kept saying it, Willa knew it wasn't her fault. But she should've been smarter. Even if it was impossible to know better, she still should've known better.

Time passed by as Willa quietly held onto Poppy's hand. Once she felt satisfied with her condition, Willa realised she should swap back with Poppy's parents again.

"Goodbye, Poppy. I'll see you soon, I promise," she whispered, kissing her on the forehead and leaving the room.

***

"For fuck's sake!" Rome kicked out in frustration, launching a chair across the kitchen floor. He hated physical displays of aggression, but this was too far.

Rome being home quickly after such a catastrophic evening was a clue to what transpired; his superiors took over once more, separating he and Charlie from the case. While the corruption didn't surprise him, Rome couldn't believe it had gotten this far.

But that's what corruption was, and now he knew there had to be a link – no doubt about it. Was it that his higher-ups were directly affiliated with the incident? Or were they wrapped around someone's finger? And if it was someone's influence, who had enough power to manipulate the police force?

A condescending blonde woman came into his mind as he remembered Penelope Quinn. It seemed she had the power, and Lachlan was linked with the masks. They'd looked into Richard, too, but no one had seen him for weeks.

Regardless, Rome knew Penelope was an integral piece of the puzzle, but what about Annabel? Did she also have sway on the police force? Or was she just working with Penelope? What motive would Annabel even have?

He also couldn't just put Annabel in jail just because she had terrible friends. Willa was her friend. He can't just arrest someone because he didn't like them, either.

He bent down and picked his chair up, putting it back in place when he heard the doorbell ring. He looked at the clock: past 11pm. No one had a reason to visit him this late. Or did they?

Rome walked to the entrance, feeling the gun in his holster, and cautiously opened the door.

Standing in front of him was Willa. Someone who gave him all the clarity he needed after such a big day. In an instant, he stopped the self-pitying because he knew however bad his day was, her day was much worse.

But before he could even invite her in, she stepped forward, swiftly placed her hands around his neck, and kissed him.

While he was shocked, it took less than a second for Rome to wrap his arms around Willa and kiss her back. This is what he'd been waiting for all along, and it was finally here.

Willa pulled back and looked at Rome's face, where he couldn't hide his confusion.

"What... was that?" he whispered, scared that she'd label it a mistake of sorts.

Willa's gut dropped thinking she may have misinterpreted everything. All this time, all of their flirtation, and now she finally broke their boundaries. Was she wrong about it all?

She stepped back nervously, taking hold of the doorknob, ready to shut herself out and off again. "I'm so sorry," she stammered.

Rome's eyes widened when he realised he'd given off the wrong impression.

"Wait!" he said, blocking the door from closing. She already began facing the other direction, ready to run, when Rome took her arm. He gently spun her back around to kiss her once more.

No longer feeling shocked, he let his tongue roam her mouth. He cradled her face with one hand and kept the other hand back around her waist in fear that she'd run out of his life forever. They pulled away only to stare deep into each other's eyes.

"You kissed me," she pointed out in a breath.

"You kissed me first," he reminded her.

Suddenly feeling embarrassed of their display on the street front, Willa blushed.

"Let's go inside," Rome chuckled.

Willa walked inside the door, and he cautiously followed after her while she took a seat on a barstool at his kitchen island.

"I didn't know you thought about me in that way," he spoke, breaking the silence.

"I… uh," she broke off, feeling embarrassed.

"Whether you're brave enough to say it right now or not, you've given me all I need to get things out in the open," he started. "I like you, Willa. Hell, I like you a lot more than that."

"Since when?" she asked.

"Much earlier than I'd like to admit," he laughed.

"And why?" she asked keenly, looking for affirmation.

Rome looked to the side, wondering why he was going along with the persistent questions. But he also wanted to make sure she knew where his head was at, in fear of a missed opportunity in the future.

"How don't you know? You're funny, so smart, and not to mention gorgeous. We've been through hell and back together. Wasn't it only a matter of time until I fell for you?"

Willa blushed, finally deciding to open up. "I like you too, Rome. A lot."

"Why?" he teased, nearing over to her, placing his arms on the island around either side of her bar stool.

"Just because you fell for that one doesn't mean I will," she teased, looking up at him.

He grinned, leaning in to kiss her on the cheek.

"Willa... I just need to be sure about something," he said.

Her brow raised, egging him to go on.

"I need to know that this isn't happening because you need someone to be on your side. At this point I'd do anything for you, but I don't want you to force yourself into something you don't want just for some support," he sighed.

Willa looked up and saw his sincerity. Now was her turn to iron out his worries.

"You asked me why – and Rome, I have so many reasons. You're always there for me, without expecting anything in return. You're great company, despite how often I pretend you aren't, and when you're not around... I won't deny that I get lonely," she breathed, tracing her fingers over his jaw.

"But why tonight? Of all times?" Rome asked. Sure, he liked where things were going, but he had to be honest, knowing it wasn't exactly the day for it.

Willa took a deep breath and a long exhale after. "Today, James told me he wanted to marry Poppy."

Rome's eyes widened as he saw her lips quiver.

"I'm not envious. I'm too young for that right now... But with what happened, we don't know if he's even going to be alright, let alone be able to tell her how he truly feels.

"And so, after seeing my best friend in hospital, and how quickly things can change, I didn't want to put up a wall anymore, Rome. I didn't want to have any unresolved feelings," she said.

Rome swallowed, playing with her fingers while she spoke.

"I want to be honest. Because if one of us got hurt, especially after a day like today, I couldn't handle knowing that I never told you how I felt about you," she said surely.

"So… What does that make us now?" Rome asked, wanting clarity before he got carried away.

"What do you want it to make us?" Willa asked, letting him take over. She said what she needed to; the ball was in his court.

"In fear of sounding like a teenager… I guess this means we're official, doesn't it?" his eyes lit up.

"I guess so," she smiled back.

Rome grinned and immediately picked Willa up off the barstool.

"Rome!" she squealed in surprise, sliding down into his arms and getting enveloped in a bear hug.

"I can't believe you've made me like you even more," he smiled and leaned in for a quick peck on the lips.

Willa frowned at the briefness of the kiss, waiting for him to explain.

"I think we should take things slowly, all things considered. We both have so much to focus on. I don't want you feeling drained by me," he said.

"I won't get drained by my boyfriend, Rome," she laughed.

Trying to hide how giddy his new title made him feel, he carefully explained his words once more. "I haven't waited all this time to rush and mess things up with you. We'll figure things out as we go, but we have all the time in the world," he said.

"In for the long-haul, hey?" she joked.

Rome's face looked shocked, and he held his heart, feigning hurt. "And you're not? What does dating mean to you, Willa?"

"I thought guys our age were afraid of commitment?" she raised her brow.

"Firstly, I'm not your age. Secondly, that's not me, so don't you worry about that," he grinned.

"I guess I'll trust you then," she smiled back. She did feel guilty that they were having such a blissful ending to a horrible day, but for the sake of them making progress on both the case and their relationship, she needed to calm down with a distraction.

Taking note that it was too late for Willa to go home, Rome put on a movie for them both and cuddled up on the couch, not knowing if he was dreaming or still awake.

When the movie reached a quiet moment, Willa spoke up.

"How did things turn out when I left?" her words were quiet, as if she were half asleep or merely sleep talking.

Rome sighed, looking down at her closed eyes. Her head was slightly resting on his chest since he had his arm around her shoulders. Despite the pressing question that reminded him of his earlier frustration, he felt relatively calm.

"They've taken us off the case; I expect another cover-up within days," he sighed.

"But we won't let that happen, will we?" she whispered through a yawn.

"We? You know that's my responsibility, right?" he reminded her.

"Not anymore," she mumbled, before drifting off completely.

Rome wasn't someone who had needed friends or attention to survive, but a strange wave of emotion rolled over him as he looked down at the sleepy girl in his arms.

"You're right, not anymore," he smiled.

Chapter Eighteen

A few days had passed since the incident, and because Rome was dealing with the aftermath, Willa found more time to herself.

And the more she was alone, the more unstable she felt. She'd taken time off class to help her recover from the trauma, and she finally decided she should see someone to help process her emotions.

After all, she couldn't talk to Poppy about it because she'd been through so much more. She also couldn't mention it to someone who wasn't involved, because like Rome had worried, it was obviously being swept under the rug.

Since the incident, there were no press conferences about it on television. Willa thought families must have been bribed to keep quiet based on the number of people paying their student loans in full when she handed in her leave slips.

Even The Bakery hadn't made an official statement about what happened on any of their social media. They owed it to the people, didn't they?

While everyone was in a wild world of secrecy, Willa knew she could count on Poppy. Nothing was keeping her quiet; no bribe would silence what happened to James. He was still in a coma recovering, and while doctors were optimistic, there's always a chance he won't wake up. But before Willa could go and talk to her, she needed to take care of herself first.

"Willa Triston? Dr. Whitman can see you now," the receptionist called out.

Willa looked up and realised where she was once more – at her local clinic. She was so lost in thought that she forgot what she was doing.

"Thank you," she acknowledged the new lady on shift, following the familiar direction down the hall to Barry's office.

"Willa, how are you?" he welcomed her warmly, despite the fact that she rejected him over text. Fortunately, even if it was just to remain composure as a professional, he wasn't holding it against her.

"Hi Barry," she said, taking a seat. "I'm actually not alright."

"Oh?" he reached for her hand to show reassurance but stopped mid-way, understanding his boundaries.

"I think I might need to talk to someone."

"What's going on?" he asked, even if it wasn't his place. But he was still her doctor, and she knew she should be able trust him.

"There was an incident at the concert I went to the other day. So many people died," her eyes welled up as she remembered the smell of people burning alive.

"Wait, what?" his eyes widened.

"I don't know why, but the people above Rome are trying to cover it up, so now no one knows about it, even though it's a mass slaughter... that's fucked up, right? There's no good, reasonable explanation for that?" she cried.

"I don't know anything about this... does that mean they sent the injured to hospitals outside of Devonthorpe?" Barry speculated, and Willa thought he didn't believe her for a moment.

But he had a point. For the first time since the incident, Willa realised that this was the closest hospital or clinic to the concert... and for some reason, Poppy wasn't escorted here.

"They're trying to keep people from Devonthorpe catching on, just like before." Willa's eyes widened. "They're going to do this again, aren't they?"

Barry looked confused, letting Willa know he didn't have the answers once more. "Are you still wanting the referral?"

Willa stood from her chair, feeling a surge of energy. Her pent-up emotions could apparently wait because getting back in the game had already consumed her.

"No… I'm seeing clear as day now," she answered, ready to go back out.

"Willa, wait!" Barry said, grabbing her hand to stop her. "I'm not trying to force you as your doctor, but as your friend, I don't want to see you burn yourself out. With whatever happened, you had the right instinct to seek help; shouldn't you go through with it?"

"I'll come back after this is all over, but now that you've given me a clue, I think I'll be okay when I figure it out," she said.

"Well, fine. But don't shut yourself off, okay? If not a doctor or a professional, talk this through with a friend at least?"

"Right… okay. I promise," she said, turning out the door.

Once Willa left the clinic, she felt her phone buzz in her pocket, and smiled when she saw Rome's name come up.

"Hey," she answered.

"Hey Willa, just wondering how you're going?" he spoke out.

Rome was someone who needed a lot of reassurance in a relationship. They hadn't seen each other since she stayed over after they first got together, and Willa could tell he was getting anxious.

Even if they both had other priorities, and they were taking it slow… she missed him.

"I'm good. I just had a check-up," she said, omitting the real reason behind it.

"Oh?" he paused. "With Barry?"

Rome felt a pang of jealousy, but he was her doctor, after all.

"The one and only. But the visit made me realise something. The victims who survived weren't transported to any nearby hospital – wouldn't that be riskier? Shouldn't they have stayed in Devonthorpe?"

"Maybe they had better equipment for the job?" he played the devil's advocate.

"No, that's the thing." Willa thought back to what had been irking her. "I remember seeing a press release last year. The Devonthorpe hospital should be the best in the area?"

"So, you're saying they didn't have their best interests in mind."

"It doesn't make sense, unless..."

"Unless they were aiming for a higher mortality rate," Rome understood her point.

"It's not just your office being manipulated. Maybe it's our medical services too?" she asked.

"We've got to find a link between who can influence all the emergency departments," he sighed. He heard traffic on the end of her phone and wondered where she was. "Are you walking home again?"

"The next bus is in an hour. I'm not waiting for that."

"And you didn't drive, why?"

"...Parking is tricky here."

"Goddamn it, Willa," he laughed. "I'll come to pick you up. I'm just on patrol now, anyway."

"No, it's okay. I'm going to head to Poppy's," she said.

"Alright, but text me when you want to go home, please. I'll pick you up after if you like."

"No need, but thank you," she smiled, ending the call not long after.

***

Willa walked the short distance to Poppy's townhouse, which was near her work at the hospital cafe. Poppy always said that she will only ever commute for one thing, not two. That meant she was using public transport for university, and for work, she could waltz out of bed five minutes before her shift started to get there in time.

Willa punched the access code into Poppy's security gate and reached the front door, giving it a few quick knocks.

"Poppy? Are you in there?" There was no response to Willa's question, but she still took the initiative to open the unlocked door and find her way inside.

Willa wandered through the house until she reached Poppy's bedroom, where she saw her bundled up in blankets, with her blinds shutting out the world.

"Hey... hey Poppy," Willa said, approaching her hazy-minded friend.

"Willa?" she sounded surprised. Her voice was hoarse from all the crying that her puffy face indicated she'd been doing.

"How are you healing up?" Willa asked. She thought there was no point asking an emotion-filled question for now. It might have been insensitive of her to say, 'how are you feeling?' if the answer was clearly not good.

"It's going well," she answered, remaining in her duvet cocoon.

They sat there in silence for a long moment until Willa eventually spoke up. "Do you mind if I sleep over?"

"Why?" Poppy whispered.

"I just want to be around you for the moment. I don't want you to be alone. I want to be that selfish," Willa answered, kicking her shoes off and jumping into the bed too.

"Sure..." Poppy whispered, before falling fast asleep.

***

When Poppy woke, she looked around and noticed a difference in her room. It was clean.

Willa had cleared out the empty chip packets that Poppy ate in her despair, and she also cleaned off an old nail polish stain from before The Bakery's concert even happened.

"Willa?" Poppy called out, looking around.

"Hey, you're awake," Willa smiled as she stepped into the bedroom.

"Yeah, what time is it?" Poppy asked. "I feel like I've slept for a week."

"It's only 11am, but from what your parents told me, you *have* slept for a week," Willa laughed.

"You spoke to them?"

"We've been keeping in touch since I visited you at the hospital."

"Oh, right…" Poppy looked down, then locked eyes again. "Willa?"

"Yeah?"

"Thank you for coming over," she said, beginning to burst into tears. Poppy finally felt comfortable enough to express how grateful she was that Willa stayed by her side, even when she wasn't up to talking.

***

"I feel like such an ass, being upset about my situation when I'm lucky enough to be alive. I should be grateful that I'm not putting my family through any more pain. I'm sounding entitled, aren't I?" Poppy asked, while eating a spoonful of ice-cream.

Willa had been consoling Poppy until deep into the afternoon before she finally had the strength to open up about her feelings on the matter. It seemed she was now bored with being sad, and she wanted to work through what had actually happened, including processing her guilt.

"Of course not! You're the loveliest person I know. You're just utterly heartbroken, since James is still in a coma." Willa said.

Poppy nodded as if to say 'true' as she shoved another spoonful into her mouth.

"Hey, I've got to tell you something," Willa continued.

"What is it?" Poppy dropped her spoon into the near-empty container and listened attentively.

"Before what happened... happened. When you went dancing at the front for a bit, James and I got talking," she explained.

"And?" Poppy frowned, not knowing what would come out of this awkward confession.

"He told me he was going to propose to you, Poppy," she said.

Poppy's mouth opened, and unlike the reaction Willa expected, her eyes remained dry. "You're kidding..."

"No, he was very excited, and he wanted to know my thoughts on it," Willa drew on, feeling an odd atmosphere unravelling. "I didn't know if I should tell you, I'm sorry for not letting you know until now, but I didn't want you to get upset while things are still up in the air."

"God..." Poppy began. "I would've said no. Fuck, I would've said no."

"What?" Willa's eyes widened.

"Well, we're so young! I couldn't get married now," she exclaimed.

"But you loved him... Right?" Willa questioned.

"Oh, absolutely. More than anything else in the world. James is my soulmate, and a part of me will feel numb until he wakes up," Poppy's eyes teared up a bit once more. "But I'm glad he didn't get the chance to ask me, because I would've said no."

Willa was momentarily stunned. She could totally understand Poppy's point about being too young, but why was she so adamant after everything that happened?

Poppy, sensing Willa's confusion, continued on. "Being who I was, carefree a week ago, I would've said no. But, if James asked me, and things turned out the way they did, I wouldn't have forgiven myself for the rest of my life. Maybe now I would say yes, because I've seen how quickly the tables can turn," she explained. "I'm making no sense, am I?" Poppy sighed, wiping her tears.

Willa took a moment to process her words, translating them to make sense in her own brain. "No, Poppy, you're right. You're more mature than I give you credit for, you know that?"

"As in, do I know you've been underestimating me? Always," she let out a soft laugh.

"Do you think you're going to be okay?" Willa asked.

"You know what? I think I am. In fact, for James' sake, I have to be," she answered. Poppy stepped up and took out her phone. "I'm ready to call his parents now. I should help them get through this too."

"I'm so proud of you, Poppy," Willa complimented, stepping up to give her a warm hug. This hug was a relief for them both. While Willa was traumatised by what she witnessed, she didn't want to burden Poppy when she was recovering from her fragile state. For the first time all week, she felt her friend would be able to get through this.

Willa's phone buzzed in her pocket, and she let go of Poppy to see who it was.

"Rome?" Poppy asked, knowing the answer already.

"Maybe?" Willa looked at the text, trying to hide her blush.

"You're finally dating, aren't you?" she smiled.

"Yeah, we are," Willa said.

"I knew it would work out, Willa," she released a healthy grin.

"Thanks, Pop. I love you," she said.

"I love you too," Poppy smiled. "Now get out of here. I have some calls to make."

"Alright, alright," Willa laughed, giving her another hug and leaving through the door.

***

Rome watched a cab pull up to the police department through his office window and out popped the very girl who didn't reply to his texts last night. Or this morning. He grinned, despite it all, as he took in her appearance. She looked nervous, but that didn't stop her rushing into the building with a smile growing on her face.

God, she was beautiful. But most of all, she looked like she was okay. He knew she was at Poppy's the night prior, and honestly, it could've gone either way for her. This was the best possible outcome, and he hoped that she got some closure. He walked to meet her out the front, where Charlie had already begun talking to her.

"Well, look who we have here," he said, patting her on her back.

She decided to get straight to the point. "Hey there. Any leads?"

"You might want to ask the boss about that one. While I like having you around the office, I still don't know how much I'm allowed to say," he said honestly.

"What's this? We're following the rules now? Damn it," she laughed.

"And what's that supposed to mean?" Rome interjected, making himself known.

"Oh? Nothing, right Charlie?" Willa grinned, nudging his deputy.

He laughed. "Yeah, what she said."

"Are you coming in?" Rome rolled his eyes, pointing toward his office.

"Bye Charlie, he's no fun," she teased.

Charlie's eyes widened at her willingness, knowing that only two weeks ago, she would've left the office waiting for Rome to chase after her. Something must have changed between them, but Rome was nice enough to not boast about it.

When they both entered the office, Rome closed the door behind them, grabbing Willa by the waist and gently setting her on his couch.

"What on earth are you doing?" she grumbled half-heartedly before Rome knelt down in front of her. He took her hand and held it to the side of his face, looking back into her eyes.

"I've missed you, Willa," he said.

She blushed, not wanting to reject him anymore.

"Do you kneel before all the girls you miss?" she raised an eyebrow.

He laughed, pulling her in for a hug. "Remind me why we haven't seen each other for a week?"

"Because you're working on the case, and I had to deal with Poppy," Willa answered, rolling her eyes.

"But that's not fair," he joked, wondering how she'd go about cheering him up. "How was your visit with Barry?"

"Oh?" she chuckled at the angle he took. "I didn't know you were such a jealous person, Rome."

"Jealous? Me?" he laughed. "Can't you change to another doctor? One that didn't try to steal you away?"

"That would be too hard for me and too easy for you," she propped herself up in her chair, staring into his eyes as if to challenge him.

The proximity blurred Rome's mindset, making his brain feel like it was bursting.

"Can I kiss you?" he whispered, looking down at her lips.

"You don't have to ask me anymore," she said with a shaky breath. He leaned in and made her lips his, slowly moving his mouth to kiss every angle of her smile.

"God, I missed you," he repeated as he sat beside her on the couch.

Willa's heart was racing a mile a minute from their brief but passionate kiss, and she tried to clear her mind. She came here for a reason, after all.

"Did you find out any leads on who could be influencing both departments?" she asked.

"Not yet for the hospital, but I've had someone in mind for a while now when it comes to the police, and I can't let this hunch get away before more people get hurt," he said.

"You think it's Penelope, don't you?"

"Isn't it the best we have at the moment?" he asked, feeling frustrated.

"It's just like Barry – you're going after anyone who uses up my time," she frowned.

"Willa, Barry is clearly different. This is about saving lives. I can't worry about niceties," he said.

"Well, I guess I shouldn't worry about you either," she gathered herself to leave.

"Willa, wait," he said.

She turned around with a tired smile. "I'm kidding, Rome. But I still don't agree with your hunch. I've met these people. So, what? Are you going to go after Annabel next? They run in the same circles."

"I will if evidence deems it necessary," he joked, despite being serious at heart… but he liked how she and him weren't letting this matter get between them.

"It's clear we have different ideas, but I'll prove they're innocent – we're wasting time looking in the wrong direction, and it's time we don't really have," she said.

"Well, off you go, detective. I'm looking forward to it," Rome chuckled as she left the room.

***

Willa was in her car, clutching at the steering wheel, wondering what she should do. She hated doubting Rome, especially as an inexperienced student who wasn't technically an investigator. Yet she still doubted him for the sake of Annabel.

Deep down, while she respected what Penelope stood for, Willa wouldn't care about protecting her if she was a part of this. But after months of torment, including being attacked by Lachlan, Willa deserved to find out for herself.

She could see from Rome's perspective; Penelope was definitely suspicious – what better way to research her than to do it through Annabel? Annabel might be the best lead they had.

Willa looked at her phone and sighed. Since the incident, dealing with Poppy's grief and her own, she didn't have the energy to be talking to Annabel like nothing had happened. Because of that, she'd ignored not one, not two, but five messages from Annabel.

Why on *earth* would she ignore her mentor? Regardless of what space she was in, Annabel was Willa's pride and joy. Without her obsession, ignoring Annabel could be bad for her career.

She clicked on Annabel's contact details and called her mobile.

"Hello? Willa?" Annabel answered in a hurry. "Are you okay?"

"Hey Annabel, yeah, I'm alright. I'm so sorry for not replying to you; it's been a really hectic week," she answered.

"Oh, don't worry about that, dear. I completely understand," Annabel gave a sigh of relief.

"Would you be free any time soon? I'd love to have a catch-up with you," Willa prompted.

"Yes, of course! What's the likelihood of you being free now?"

Willa's eyes widened, surprised by her eagerness – but she was more than excited about the proposition.

"I'm not busy at all!" she answered a little too keenly. "Where would you like to meet?"

"Why don't you come over to my house for afternoon tea? I've wanted to spend some time with you for a while now."

"I'd love to. I'll be there in thirty minutes," Willa said, ending the call afterwards.

With all this excitement, she almost forgot the plan, and she needed to get back on track. Willa plugged her phone into the aux cord and put some music on, pulling out of the station parking lot and starting her journey.

***

Like Willa promised, it only took her half-an-hour to get to Annabel's gorgeous home. As the gates opened, Willa took a moment to admire the garden that was even more overgrown than her last visit, before knocking on the door.

Unlike the first time Willa visited, it wasn't Annabel's butler that opened the door – it was Annabel herself.

"Willa! Darling, come here!" Annabel said, bringing her in for a warm hug.

Willa was confused by the overfamiliarity, but maybe she and Annabel really were that close?

"Hi, thanks for inviting me over," Willa said meekly.

Willa trailed Annabel's footsteps to a lounge room with a big charcuterie board on the coffee table. There were vegan cheeses, crackers, and an assortment of pureed vegetables to dip into.

"I hope you're hungry. We have quite a bit of food to get through here," Annabel grinned.

"I am actually, so this is perfect," Willa sat down on a beige cushioned armchair while Annabel sat on a navy loveseat. Willa reached for some cheese and a cracker to buy her some time when thinking about where to start.

Firstly, she needed to clear Annabel of any suspicion, and she could do this perfectly through a pitiful apology.

"Great. I thought I'd prep something quickly for you since you said you were having a rough week… did you want to talk about it?" she smiled politely, helping Willa by getting right on topic.

"Yeah, if you don't mind… I witnessed a major incident on Tuesday, and it really rattled me. My friends got hurt, too." Willa sighed.

"Tuesday, you say. What happened? Weren't you at the student conference?" Annabel's brow shot up.

"Actually, I was at The Bakery's concert," Willa admitted. Annabel's eyes widened, waiting for her to go on.

"I had already bought tickets before you asked about meeting up. I'm so sorry I lied to you," she said.

"Willa…" Annabel took a moment to sigh and reclaim a neutral face. "So then, what happened?"

"You didn't hear?" Willa tested.

"Hear what?" Annabel continued, looking confused.

Willa felt a sense of relief, almost mad at herself for suspecting someone as wonderful as Annabel. It was an unjustly buried case, so if she knew what happened, that meant she would have to be involved somehow. But she didn't know, and Willa could rest easy.

Instead, Willa could actually use Annabel as the pillar of support that she'd offered to be since they met.

"There was some kind of electrical surge, and it killed so many people," she started.

"What? Oh, Willa!" Annabel said, rushing over and leaning beside her for support.

"My best friend Poppy was electrocuted, and her boyfriend was trampled in the panic," Willa started to weep, feeling heard. Sure, Rome was definitely there for her, but he also had to deal with what happened too. And Willa was too busy being there for Poppy for her to switch the roles.

"I cannot believe this…" Annabel sighed, frowning with a distant emotion in her eyes. She quickly turned it to rage. "How did I not know about this? How does anyone not know about this?"

"I don't know!" Willa exclaimed. "That's the thing, someone is burying it, and even the police station is having to let it all go."

"Did Sheriff Pendleton tell you this?" she asked.

"Yep, he's dealing with a lot at the moment – you can tell he's feeling guilty about it all," she admitted. Rome hated things happening on his watch, and they'd been one step behind throughout this whole case.

"We need to uncover this, Willa," Annabel asserted.

"Should we?" Willa frowned, wondering about the implications of going public.

"Absolutely. If that many lives are at stake, and if you think more people might be at risk, then we need to get it out there," she said.

"You're right, but how?" Willa asked. Rome didn't specifically say she had to keep it under wraps, he was just worried about her being a target.

"Just you wait, I'll get someone on it as soon as possible, and we'll have a press conference in no time. What else has Rome told you? What do you know?" Annabel asked.

"Well, we know it's linked to Ron and Dave Donohugh, some electricians who were working on the wires without permission a few months ago," she said.

"Wow, first the carbon footprint, and now this. Electricians truly are the worst," Annabel tried to lift Willa's spirit with the joke but realised now wasn't the time. "That's a brilliant piece of information to narrow down the demographic."

"These people also run around in masks," Willa continued.

"Oh? And you know this how?"

"Remember Lachlan? When the school shut down? Well, he had the same mask, and I also saw the culprits wearing them at the concert," she answered.

"What? You saw them?" Annabel asked sharply.

"Just one person's real face... it was Joe Mark, someone who I knew because they worked with Rome. He was fired," Willa said.

Annabel turned still as stone. "We can definitely expose that. What else?"

"How well do you know Penelope Quinn?" Willa questioned.

"What?"

"Rome thinks she's somehow a part of this, but his team doesn't know how just yet," Willa baited.

"I'm sure he's mistaken – Penelope has always been an outstanding citizen!" Annabel said, shocked.

"I think so too. You're saying you'd vouch for her?" Willa said, eyeing Annabel. She stopped for only a split second before answering.

"You know what? No... I guess I wouldn't."

"So, he might be right. I'm sorry for dragging your friend into this," Willa said.

"No friend of mine would be involved in this," Annabel said nobly.

"We'll figure this out, Annabel, I promise," Willa said, feeling confident.

"I'll be here to help in any way. In the meantime, I'll deal with Penelope and see what she's up to," she said.

"Just make sure to keep it between us until we know for sure," Willa reminded.

"Of course," Annabel smiled, changing the subject to something lighter.

Chapter Nineteen

I
t had only been a day since Willa visited Annabel. They wanted to expose the situation diplomatically, where the victims won't be triggered by the horrors that had transpired.

Willa was grateful that in a time like this, she had someone like Annabel to rely on. She sat in bed, staring up at her ceiling, wondering what they could truly do to bring justice to the town and get rid of the corruption. But the truth is, Willa still felt like a child. What good ideas could she possibly come up with to stop something of this magnitude?

This wasn't a young adult television show where all the high school characters have the power to rise up against the bad guy. Rome didn't even have authority as the town Sheriff.

Willa's phone began to buzz. Spotting Rome's name on the caller ID, she answered.

"Good morning," she spoke with a tired voice.

"Willa, turn on the TV right now. Put on the local news," Rome said abruptly.

"Huh? Why?" she queried, startled by his urgency.

"Just do it, Willa!" he prompted.

While she didn't enjoy the attitude, she knew it must have been important.

Willa walked to the lounge room of her apartment and grabbed the remote, turning the television on. She watched the local news late last night, so she didn't need to search for the channel.

But what she saw shocked her. Standing next to the local news reporter Michelle Mathers, she saw two people she knew well.

It was Leonard and Rachel, Poppy's parents.

"What are they doing?" she spoke aloud.

"Just watch," Rome replied.

"We're devastated; our daughter went to the hospital, along with so many others… some who did survive and some who didn't. But what's been done about it? Who knew about it? Not even our neighbours!" Rachel wept while Leonard kept her steady.

The screen switched to a vision of the concert arena, where phone footage showed what had gone down that day. People were screaming, running away from the areas where people had dropped down, either dead or injured.

"They're showing it," Willa looked on.

The screen shot back to Michelle, but this time she wasn't with Poppy's parents.

"There's been a major media block about the terrors that went down last Tuesday. It wasn't until the victims approached us that we even knew what happened," she spoke.

"But while this is a devastating time, local celebrity activist Annabel Hale has some information that you won't want to miss," Michelle said, walking towards Willa's mentor.

"Oh my god," Willa's eyes widened.

"This is a major disservice to the people. We deserve to know what happens in our community. When such tragedy occurs, servicemen like the local police force are responsible for keeping us safe and informed," she said.

"So, you believe the focus should be on the malpractice of the police?" Michelle asked.

"Absolutely. It's corrupt. Countless youth have died, and many victims were silenced. For what? That's what I would like to know," Annabel answered.

After a slight pause, she continued. "Perhaps it's not out of malice, but out of a lack of competence. I'm calling out the local Sheriff, Rome Pendleton, as he knew what happened and didn't inform the public for their safety."

Willa's heart stopped hearing an uncomfortable intake of breath over the phone. Annabel was naming and shaming. She thought she knew the whole picture, but apparently, she didn't. How didn't she understand what Willa tried to tell her?

"That's all for now; I'm Michelle Mathers and this is Devonthorpe News."

The program moved on to an advertisement, and Willa turned the television off.

"Rome, I'm so sorry," Willa said, noticing her hands starting to shake.

"Why did she do this? Did she know all along?" Rome said, suspecting Annabel.

"No, this is all my fault. I spoke to her yesterday. I tried to leak information to trick her into talking about Penelope, but I think she didn't understand what I was saying," Willa's voice shook.

"Willa…" Rome let out a disappointed sigh.

"People should know about this, she was right in doing so, but she's twisted the focus so much," Willa uttered quickly.

"This is really going to complicate things. What happens when Penelope sees this? She's going to double down." Rome expressed.

"Well, that's what I don't understand… When I spoke to Annabel, I told her about how we thought Penelope was involved. I told her that Joe was there at the scene, and all about the people with masks," Willa spoke quickly. "But she didn't mention any of that?"

Rome let out another sigh after thinking for a moment. "It's a tricky situation. She's either dumber than you thought, where her sway is harmful to us because of her lack of interpretation, or she's purposely diverting the information. Did she know you were there that day?"

Willa hated doubting her, but Rome's points were spot on. "No, I told her I was somewhere else," she answered.

"Maybe she thought it was all wrapped up until she found out you were digging around, and that's what called for the shift of focus?"

"If she's reporting this, why would she be in on it? Wouldn't that be worse for her, outing her own crimes on live TV?"

"I don't know, Willa. I just need us to be open to all possibilities," Rome said. He paused for a moment, and Willa could hear an incoming call on his end. "I've got to go. Charlie is on the next line."

"Rome… I'm so, so sorry."

"You're fine, Willa. We'll work through this together," he reassured her, ending the call shortly after.

***

Rome was sat at his kitchen island, trying not to shake with anxiety. He was resilient, but this turn of events was detrimental to both his work and their advantage. Before he lost all hope, Charlie called.

"Rome speaking," he answered.

"I'm guessing you saw what happened?"

"Yeah, it's a goddamn train wreck," he sighed.

"What are we going to do? If our higher-ups aren't liking what's happening, given the fact that they're the ones who buried it, we're gonna cop the brunt of it," Charlie panicked.

"Don't worry, I'll be the one getting the brunt of it, not you," Rome sighed.

"What can we do to stop that? Because without you on the case, nothing is going to get done. Who knows who will get targeted next?" Charlie's voice elevated.

"It's alright; we need to be smarter. But yes, something *will* happen because of this, and we need to be prepared," Rome said.

"What do you mean?"

"If you think about it, they're going to fire me. They have to. But if I step down, and you go in my place..." Rome started.

"No, I couldn't! I wouldn't know how to be a Sheriff. Besides, you don't deserve that."

"Even just temporarily, then. Until we get this all sorted. If you take over, the media will make it seem like I'm out of the picture, but we can work in the background together. We can figure it out without the world knowing." Rome explained.

"Do you really think we could pull off something like that?" Charlie asked.

"It'll be simple enough, I just have to stay out of the picture, and you'll need to keep a level head... but there are some things I want to figure out. I'll need time to work on this," Rome said.

"What do you mean? With Annabel?"

"Well, yes, eventually... but first I need to go out of town and see if there are links with this happening elsewhere. We need help, Charlie, and I'll be the one to find it."

"If you say so. Well, I guess I'll hold the fort until then?" Charlie wanted confirmation.

"Yes, thank you, Charlie. You're a great friend."

"You too, Rome. You know that."

Rome ended the call, leaving Charlie alone at the other end of the line.

***

Charlie almost felt sick knowing that Rome wouldn't be coming in that day. They betrayed him. When he was trying to stop it all, Annabel made him sound at fault.

Charlie sighed, knowing his wife wouldn't be too happy with his promotion. Too far away from home for too long, he thought. But it was his duty now, and this wasn't the type of job you'd just quit. They both had responsibilities they'd taken upon themselves, above and beyond what their superiors demanded.

A bell's jingle at the door caught Charlie's attention, where he saw a man in a dark suit enter. He'd seen photos of this man before but never saw him in person. Charlie gulped, knowing he'd need to be strong to get through this lie.

The man cleared his throat as he approached Charlie's bench.

"My, Commissioner John Foyer in our small little district! I feel honoured, sir," Charlie feigned cleverly.

"No need, no need. Now…" he looked down at Charlie's name badge. "Charlie, sir."

"Charlie, do you know if the Sheriff is in?" his eyes squinted.

"Well, funny that. I'm sure you saw this morning's broadcast, sir?" Charlie asked.

"Yes, I did."

"It's quite an embarrassment to the station, isn't it? Well, Rome resigned accordingly. I'm the new person in charge if that's alright with you?" Charlie explained.

"Well, what better than someone from the area to take over," he smiled.

Charlie could tell he was pleased with Rome's decision to resign, and that he didn't have to fire someone today.

"I guess I'll let you carry on – I need to work on some PR issues, as you can imagine. I'll announce you as the new head of the station while I'm at it."

"Excellent, sir. Thank you for your visit," Charlie smiled a tight lip smile.

"No, thank you, Sheriff," he winked, walking back out the door where he came from.

Charlie released a breath he didn't know he was holding and eyed the door until it shut. "Prick."

***

After she got off the phone with Rome, Willa had begun driving to Devonthorpe Park. It was where Annabel's interview took place, and she recognised the scenery in the background.

When she arrived, she parked her car and stormed out. She wasn't a confrontational person, and especially not to people she respected, but what had just happened?

Willa spotted Annabel just in time, as she was about to get into her vehicle. "Annabel!" Willa called out.

She looked back, pausing when she saw Willa, and then opened with a bright smile. "Oh, Willa! It's nice to see you here."

"What was that?" Willa frowned as she approached her.

"Oh, I said it's nice to see you here," she feigned innocence.

"No, I meant the broadcast. Why didn't you tell me about it?" Willa started.

"There's a big rush when it comes to these things. After you told me about Poppy, I had to get in touch with her family to help break the news," she said simply.

"But Poppy wouldn't have wanted to be used like this, Annabel," Willa glowered.

"I don't think she'd mind when there's so much at stake."

"But what's at stake for you? Why did you go after Rome like that? That's not what I told you…" Willa demanded.

Annabel sighed, placing her keys in her pocket, before taking on a happy face again. She placed a hand on Willa's back and guided her forward. Willa, for the first time, didn't enjoy Annabel's warm touch. She felt it came from a devious place.

"I think we should talk about this in depth. Let's grab a coffee, shall we?" Annabel said, but she wasn't asking.

A wave of disappointment washed over her, but Willa followed on. For the first time, Willa saw what Rome had seen. Annabel was someone so used to getting her way that she'd toy with Willa over such an important matter. Annabel ushered Willa into a small coffee shop with one empty table and told her to have a seat. Willa did, realising Annabel was ordering for her. She came back to the table with two ice teas, but Willa didn't like iced tea. Despite her thinking otherwise, they didn't know each other well at all. Willa drank it anyway, but as she began to have a bitter taste in her mouth, the bitterness spread over to Annabel, too.

***

Though it was still morning, Rome had already arrived at Rosewood, the nearest town with a functioning police station. He approached the office, opened the door and looked around, hoping to see an old friend. Kathy Green, a Rosewood Officer, was handling the desk. She looked surprised to see him, then happy, and then filled with pity. "Morning, Kathy. I guess you've seen the broadcast," he joked, approaching her bench.

"The nerve that woman had," she sighed. "But I hate to ask, is it true? What happened?"

"If you don't know, you mustn't be experiencing it over here then," he answered.

"Experiencing what?" she frowned.

Rome filled Kathy in on all the details, everything from the rogue electricians to the recent mass murder.

"So, they're burying it then? I can't believe it!" Kathy exclaimed. "Something is definitely going on, and I feel like our Commissioner might be involved too," he stated.

"Well, he'd have to be – he has the power to hide things, after all," Kathy took a moment to think. "But if he's hiding it, why would he want it leaked to the public?"

"That came solely from Annabel Hale. Because of her, they made me resign. I heard from Charlie that the Commissioner himself checked that I wasn't there anymore."

"They're taking you out of the picture, Rome. I just know it," Kathy said.

"You might be right about that," he sighed. Kathy dragged him over to a quieter room as she heard some people buzzing around outside. According to Kathy, taking care of their local petty crimes could wait.

"You must have been close enough to make them nervous," she decided. "What does your gut tell you?"

Rome sat back and thought for a long while about all the pieces.

"Annabel Hale is at the centre of all this. She has to be," Rome frowned, not knowing why it made sense but knowing it had to be the answer.

"Why, though? My Sheriff would happily get involved, but not without reason," Kathy sighed.

"She's friends with Penelope Quinn, someone I can link to the corruption of the police. Annabel's using me as a scapegoat... she's got influence with our Mayor wrapped around her finger... but most importantly, she's linked to Willa."

"And who is Willa?" Kathy eyed.

"She's... she's been working on the case with me, and Annabel definitely knows how close we are. She took advantage of it with the news report; she's using her. I can feel it," he explained.

Kathy looked worried for a moment. She could see that Rome

must've been passionate about Willa, but why get her involved?

"How did she get on the case, Rome?"

"Well, Charlie arrested Willa when he found her at a crime scene. She was running from him, and he thought she was the culprit," he explained. "When she was arrested, Joe... you remember how Joe was. He took things way too far, so I fired him before we had a lawsuit on our hands. Willa was interested in the case, so I let her stick around under my supervision."

"And where's Joe now?"

"When we took him off the team, he turned bad. He was definitely involved in the concert incident," Rome said.

"So, just so I understand it all... Charlie found Willa at a crime scene, she got onto the case because Joe hurt her, Joe ended up being bad, Annabel is leaking important information you've uncovered, and now you suspect Annabel," Kathy summarised.

Rome frowned, not knowing where she was going with this.

"You're blind in love, aren't you?" Kathy sighed.

"What are you trying to say?"

"Willa's a rat, Rome. She has to be! It's all too coincidental," Kathy decided.

Rome stood up, shaking his head.

"Kathy, this isn't a joke," he said.

"Look, Rome. We'll be here for you. Annabel has clearly compromised the case; just tell us what you need, and I'll make sure the Sheriff helps... But if things turn out the way I think they might, we're going to have to take Willa in, too," Kathy explained.

Rome paused, not wanting to give the possibility a second thought. "I'll let you know our plan of action, and as for Willa, you have nothing to worry about," he said.

"I'll leave it to you, for now," Kathy let out a worried sigh. She gave him a hug goodbye and then went back behind her desk. "Good luck until then."

"Yes, thanks for hearing me out," Rome said, giving a grateful smile and exiting the Rosewood precinct.

He thought back to what Kathy said about Willa, and his skin crawled. It couldn't be possible, not at all. But it made him worry – was he that captivated by her when they first met, that he didn't catch onto a hidden motive? No, it wasn't possible. She wasn't capable of hurting people like this.

Just think about it; even her friend was affected by what happened at the stadium. There was no way she could be behind that... As for Joe, he wasn't smart enough to devise something so elaborate. They couldn't be working together. Not a chance.

But while Rome got back into his car and started his journey back to Devonthorpe, he couldn't help but feel doubtful. A feeling he never wanted Willa to know he had.

***

Annabel was sitting on the other end of the cafe table, waiting for Willa to explain what was so wrong with what she had done that morning. She fluttered her eyes, waiting expectantly for Willa's response.

"Annabel, this was... this was a breach of trust. You didn't need to go after Rome. He's doing the best he can to solve all of this," Willa explained.

Annabel leaned forward, slightly moving away from her perfect posture.

"Well, I'm truly sorry that you feel like that. I thought it was the perfect way to pick things up again," she explained.

"Pick things up? What do you mean?" Willa eyed her.

"Well, clearly, things were at a standstill, were they not?"

"No, they weren't. We were closer than ever without this... In fact, we had suspects... but why didn't you bring those suspects up? Did you even think about Penelope's actions first? Why lash out at Rome when she's clearly involved?" Willa challenged.

"Now, Willa, you're acting a bit hysterical. Don't you think? Penelope is too well known to be a part of this. What good would it be for her to get involved?" she tested.

"She freed the man who attacked me, Annabel... the man who was wearing the same mask those people have worn for months!" Willa raised her voice, drawing the attention of other diners in the cafe.

"I can see how you might think that." Annabel said.

"Stop that! Enough with these statements that make it feel like I'm confused. It's not that 'I think that'; it's factual. It's what happened," Willa started up again.

As her faith lessened in Annabel being the great, understanding mentor she once had, a foggy cloud lifted from her eyes.

"So, you're saying she's too rich to be a bad person? Is that your alibi too?" Willa continued offhandedly, until she thought for a moment about her words. She remembered what the electricians were saying to each other when she spied on them the second time. She had a voice recording to prove it... they were offered a large sum of money.

If anything, having money made someone more likely to be involved. Willa didn't know why she began suspecting Annabel, but she couldn't stop once she'd started.

In a flustered rush, Annabel didn't reply but instead stood from her seat. She nodded to her left and walked outside.

Willa chased her, ready to demand answers. A customer followed them out of the cafe, but Willa didn't care who heard what she was about to say. Annabel slipped into a small alleyway next door and stared plainly at her young protégé.

g,

Willa jolted at the sudden stop and her instincts led her to say something she couldn't take back. "You're in on this whole thing aren't you?"

Chapter Twenty

Annabel didn't give a second thought to answer Willa's accusation and instead nodded to something, or someone behind Willa.

After a sudden thump, Willa fell to the ground. Behind where she landed stood the man at fault. He'd struck her with the back of his gun and placed it back into his holster.

"Thank you, John. It was getting a bit loud, wasn't it?" she composed herself, looking over to the Commissioner.

"I couldn't agree more," he answered.

Annabel looked around outside the alleyway, waiting for a break in foot traffic.

"We're good," she said, stepping out from her own shadow. She bent down, helping John hitch Willa up in a piggy-back position and stepped guiltlessly out into public. It was almost the look of a father and his grown-up, lazy daughter.

Annabel made aimless, light conversation to lead any suspicion away from their interaction until they reached the car.

Opening up the backseat, John prepared to throw Willa inside.

"Stop!" Annabel squealed out. "Be gentle. She's still my favourite student, John."

"Oh, forgive me," he laughed ironically, doing as he was told.

Annabel then took out her phone, dialling her dear friend's number.

"Penelope? Yes, it's Annabel. I'm afraid we're going to have to speed things up. Willa has caught on."

***

Willa's eyes opened and closed hazily until she finally came to. She found herself at a familiar dining table – the one from Annabel's house, and for a second, she wondered how she got there.

Letting her eyes roam around some more, she looked down to see her arms tied to the chair she was sitting in. Willa attempted to kick her legs in a panic and realised they were also tightly bound.

She continued jolting around, finally remembering what had gone down before she passed out. Annabel kidnapped her; there's no other way to see it.

Hearing the noise Willa was making, Annabel hurried into the room. She looked as wonderful as ever and seemed sincerely concerned.

"Oh, dear! Don't move around like that. You might fall and hurt yourself," she said, rushing to steady Willa in her chair.

"You! What did you do?" Willa's eyes widened, ignoring her ingenuine kindness.

"Ah, I think you're clever enough to piece that one together yourself now, aren't you? You pieced everything else together, after all," Annabel dared to laugh, patting Willa on her forearm.

"I can't believe it... Rome was right," Willa let her jaw drop.

"Yes, well, that was our first misstep. Turns out our small-town Sheriff was much more capable than we thought... but that's all dealt with now, since we shamed him into resigning," Annabel spoke with what she thought was modesty.

"Who else was in on this? You can't have been the only one," Willa tried to dig deeper.

"Well, if you only waited a moment, I would've told you, silly!"

197

she grinned, and for the first time, Willa felt like Annabel truly was unhinged. "Time to come out, she's awake!"

A bustle of noise approached the dining room, with casual conversation coming from voices she'd heard before. As they chatted and walked on, Willa saw Penelope, Florence and her partner Xavier amongst other familiar faces in Annabel's entourage.

"Willa, how kind of you to join us," Xavier smiled.

"What's going on here?" Willa demanded. She was caught. She couldn't do anything about it, so she might as well use her time wisely.

"Annabel, I thought she was supposed to be bright," Penelope huffed.

"Penelope, be kind. Willa is our special guest, remember?" Annabel chipped.

"Well, get on with it, then," Penelope rolled her eyes and took a seat at the head of the table. The group followed her lead, filling the other chairs.

"Now, I need you to keep an open mind here, alright?" Annabel said, looking down at Willa.

"What have you done?" Willa whispered, afraid of what she'd find out.

"We're saving the world, Willa," Annabel said with a charming tone, looking around the room as her groupies cheered at the idea.

Annabel stood up and began pacing about the room as she began. "Do you know what the root of our environmental crisis is?"

Willa hated her rhetoric, but she still answered. She wanted to speed up the process of Annabel's monologue, even if it meant playing her game.

"You're practising eugenics, aren't you?" Willa's eyes narrowed.

It was a cliché, she thought. How typical for people to use overpopulation as the main problem, when there were so many smaller stage solutions that could keep everyone safe.

"Eugenics? Now, Willa. How daft do you think I am?" Annabel

laughed.

"Then what?" Willa grew impatient.

"Well, maybe you're half right. It's true, we're cleaning up some of the population around here. But not for population control," Annabel explained, picking up a vase and then throwing it at the wall in anger. "I can't stand thinking about this!"

Willa remained silent during Annabel's sudden outburst, allowing space for her to keep talking.

"This stupid, little town is the scum of the earth. Do you know why that is, Willa?" she asked, without expecting a response. "There are several peer-reviewed academics in this local area, all who think they know what they're talking about. Well, they're wrong, Willa, especially Hobbs."

Willa thought back to when the university was being attacked and remembered that Professor Hobbs was a target. More pieces of the puzzle connected as Annabel revealed her vendetta.

"I submitted a thesis – a genius plan to advance our environmental endeavours, only for my science to be deemed 'unrealistic', 'uninspired' and 'incorrect'. How dare they think so lowly of me?" she shouted, earning grunts of approval from her entourage.

"What, so you're going to kill people for it? You're murderers!" Willa seethed.

"Oh, Willa, you're so naïve. In this world, when people say you're wrong when you know you're right – you don't back down. That review almost ruined my career – people thought I was a sham! But I only need Hobbs' signature to make it all right," she explained. "With one signature, people outside of Devonthorpe will go along with my plan, without being aware of the struggle I had to go through in this putrid little town. That's a signature I'm prepared to forge, and I'll cover my tracks by getting rid of the rest of them."

"This makes no sense!" Willa spat.

"Oh, but it does! You of all people should know. What about your essay, Willa? Wiping out predators to save an ecosystem, that's all we're doing here! Imagine this town having a clean slate, with everyone going along with a plan that will protect our earth. All signs point to you being on our side," Annabel smirked.

And Willa finally realised it. She wasn't as special as she thought. She was a tool. Annabel chose her essay for the golden dinner to seek an ally, not because of her talents in writing or environmentalism.

But more than anything, she was able to see that Annabel was a hypocrite. "You want to save the world? Take a look in the mirror, Annabel. If your logic is so foolproof how come you're being an environmental hypocrite. Your mansion is a black hole for energy."

"When we're the ones cleaning the slate, we get to reap the benefits," Penelope chipped in cruelly.

"You really think that's okay? How can you live with yourselves?" Willa's lip quivered slightly.

"Now, now, Willa. It's important to look at the grand scheme of things," Annabel said, leaning down to Willa's side once more.

"I can't believe I ever trusted you..." Willa whispered, looking into her eyes.

"But there's the thing; you did. You didn't just trust me; you idolised me. You envied me. You wanted to be me," Annabel gloated, and Willa's stomach sunk at the truth. "But even now, Willa, you still can be. You can be like all of us," she said.

"Just join our cause, and you'll be safe too, Willa," Penelope spoke up again.

"And what? Leave everyone to die just so I can be safe?" Willa seethed.

"You'll be letting them make a sacrifice for the greater good," Penelope replied.

"You're all insane. Narcissistic, god complex people, who became sociopathic murderers. Do you understand that you're killing so many people who weren't even involved? Saying it's the whole damn town to justify your actions. You can't keep distancing yourself from this," she began to cry out.

"Willa... if that's the way you'd like to see it, then I understand. But you can change your mind at any time," Annabel smiled, placing her hand on Willa's shoulder to comfort her.

Willa felt cold shivers run down her spine as if Annabel's hands belonged to death itself, and her shoulder jolted as hard as she could to shrug her off. Annabel stepped back in surprise instead of steadying her like she had done previously. Willa capitalised on this small moment of freedom, causing the chair to hit the floor on its side.

She briefly hit her head before extending her arms and realising the impact had broken the chair, allowing Willa to unravel her hands and legs.

"Damn it, Willa, that was a one-of-a-kind chair," Annabel sighed, instinctively lending out a hand to help Willa up. But Annabel was wrong if she thought Willa would stay still or obedient.

Willa kicked Annabel's legs as she approached, earning a brief shriek from Annabel. Being opportunistic, Willa got up and made the most of her newfound distance.

"Willa, there's no need to be barbaric!" Annabel scolded, and those at the table stood up attentively.

Willa grabbed a broken-off chair leg from beneath her, using it as a weapon, swinging it around to establish her own perimeter.

"Really, I hoped it wouldn't come to this," Annabel sighed, still remaining calm and collected. "Joe, come in, please."

As Willa looked around, feeling angry and confused, another familiar face walked into the room. Joe Mark, with a sinister grin on his face.

"Now, would you please contain her? I think the rest of us need some air," Annabel sighed, as if she'd been hard done by from the events at hand. She left the room, and everyone but Joe followed.

Fewer people meant a greater chance of escape for Willa, and she kept her eyes peeled for any possible exits. But it was also Joe, someone who, while she hated that it gave him power, she was terrified of.

"Great to see you again, Willa," he devilishly stepped forward.

"Don't come any closer!" Willa shouted, looking around helplessly.

"I've been waiting to teach you a lesson for a long time now... last time was a treat, but it wasn't enough," he laughed, making Willa squirm.

"You should feel sick thinking of all the people you killed," she grimaced.

But as Willa thought about Joe's taunts, she had a helpful epiphany. There was a reason he wasn't given much authority at Rome's station... he wasn't reliable. Not just because he was irrational, but because he was incapable. Annabel wouldn't know this... but Willa knew how easily Joe could be provoked by his ego. He was trying to intimidate her, and Willa knew she had to get into his head if she wanted to get out of there.

"I've been sleeping like a baby. They were easy to dispose of without feeling anything," he sneered. He was enjoying this.

"Oh? Like you were at the station?" Willa began, stepping forward bravely. Joe stood in front of an open window, where Willa knew the road was nearby. She could hear cars going past, even through the hedges around the property.

Joe made a noise in his throat, finding the words to fire back, but Willa knew which direction she needed to take. "You thought I wormed my way in, wrapping Rome around my fingers as if it were some elaborate plot... But you didn't get to see how simple that was. I just had to bat my lashes and blush, then he was mine and you were out on the streets."

"You dirty bitch," Joe spat, walking closer to her.

"You were so replaceable. It didn't take any effort to keep you away for good," she smirked.

Joe rushed towards her, violently raising his hand, but she ducked under him instead. His momentum kept him hurling forward, while Willa now had a clear path to the window. She sprinted as fast as she could, hoisting her legs up and launching herself outside – only to topple down, landing on her back. She was winded, but she didn't have time to catch her breath. Instead, she used the rest of the air in her lungs to pull herself back onto her feet and ran on sheer willpower. She used the wooden chair leg to separate the hedge in front of her, leaving a clear path to burst through, but not without gaining some scratches in the process.

She kept her momentum, scrambling onto the road from the other side of the hedge, only just in time for a truck approaching.

"STOP!" she screamed, closing her eyes and hoping that as she heard the driver step on the breaks, it would stop before it got to her.

She took a second, realising she was still alive and opened her eyes.

"What are you doing?" a burly man shouted from his vehicle as Willa raced to his window.

"I need a lift, it's urgent! I'm in danger!"

The man looked around, worried for a moment, then nodding his head. "Quick, hop in. I'll take you where you need to go."

***

Willa saw Rome's house in the distance and alerted the driver. He was a cautious man, and he didn't want to know a lot about Willa's situation. He didn't even want to know her name and didn't tell her his in return. All that mattered to his conscience was that he knew he'd taken someone in danger to a safer place.

The car pulled over on the side of the road. "I hope you'll be alright," he said.

"Thank you for this," she said gratefully, hopping out of the high-set door and landing on safer ground.

***

After Rome had spoken with Kathy, Rosewood's finest, he had called Willa an umpteenth number of times, but she wasn't answering. And this radio silence caused him to do the worst – he suspected her. He was being influenced by Kathy's distrust, whether he liked it or not.

He sighed, holding his head. It had just been one day – he's sure it would all turn out okay. She's just busy; she has nothing to hide.

Breaking his train of thought, his doorbell rang. With this morning's commotion, he couldn't help but feel anxious about who it might be – it could be the Commissioner, it could be journalists haggling for a response, or it could be Charlie checking in. He hoped it was Charlie out of the lot.

He looked over his attire, making sure he was ready to be seen by anyone, and walked toward the door. He looked through the keyhole and saw none other than Willa. His heart sank.

He opened the door in a rush, seeing that she was covered in scratches and a bruise was forming on the side of her head.

"Willa?" he showed his surprise.

"Rome," she leaned in for a comforting hug.

He stood for a second, holding her before that toxic feeling arose once more. "What happened? I called you."

"I don't have my phone… they took it," she sighed, standing back.

"Who?"

"Rome, I was kidnapped. I escaped from Annabel's house and just hitchhiked here. You were right – I now know what they're up to," she said.

"How'd you manage that?" he asked pointedly.

Willa frowned. "I ran away?"

"But how?"

"I'll tell you, but what's with your tone?"

"I just... visiting Rosewood today gave me a fresh perspective. One of the officers there believes there's a weird connection between you and what's going on. There's just too many coincidences," he stated, knowing he'd be losing his edge, but wanting to give her the benefit of the doubt.

"Oh, for fuck's sake, Rome. You think I'm a part of this, don't you?"

"No, no! Believe me, I don't... or I'd like to think that isn't the case," he answered honestly.

"Don't you trust me?" she asked.

"This isn't about trust when lives are at stake, you know that Willa," he sighed guiltily.

She paused, walking over to his kitchen and pulling out a bottle of water from the fridge. She drank it as Rome simply looked on.

"I freed myself from being tied to a chair and escaped because Joe was left in charge. You know what Joe's like, ambitious but unable to deliver. I jumped out the window. I ran through the hedges, got scratched up, and leapt in front of a truck. I'm lucky the driver stopped, because I didn't know how far Joe was behind me." She raised the bottle up for another sip.

"Willa... shit, I'm so sorry," Rome said, walking forward to her again. But Willa stood back, deflecting his apology. He didn't trust her – she'd gone through hell that morning, and he could only suspect her.

"I get it, Rome. I get it, but you're all I have," Willa started, breaking down. "I can't bring this to Poppy, it's going to get her involved, and it's way too close to home."

"Willa, I know, I know, I'm so sorry," Rome stepped forward, taking her into his arms gently while she cried. His heart sank as once again he realised how fragile she was. Up close her bruise looked painful; her head would've been throbbing, for sure. He kissed her forehead as if to kiss it better. "Do you need pain killers?"

"No, it'll be fine... we need to get to work on this," she sighed, pulling away again.

They went into his home office, which had a very similar vibe to his office at work. They both took a seat and Willa began to share what she knew.

"I was kidnapped because I figured it out. Like you thought, Annabel is involved. So, I went to scold her about the broadcast and she couldn't give me a straight answer," she started. "When I said my suspicions out loud, she took me outside where someone followed and hit me over the head."

"Willa, I'm so sorry to leave you alone like that," Rome said, but Willa continued on.

"They took me to her house, and the whole environmental team was there, including Penelope. They're killing people because of a grudge, and to clear Annabel's reputation; that's literally all it is," Willa raised her voice.

"You can't be serious..."

"Dead serious. They gave me a choice – join them or burn with the others. Rome, we have to stop them," she panicked.

"We need to find out where they'll hit next and then catch them in the act. The Rosewood team is on board and aren't under the control of the Commissioner, unlike everyone else. They won't expect it, especially with me having publicly resigned," he explained.

"I think we need to take another look at the blueprints and try to figure out where they'll target next," Willa stated. "Hell, we've probably lost control of it all, since we literally handed it to corrupt police to guard."

"They're still in my office at the station," Rome said, picking up his phone and calling his old work. "Hey, Charlie, can you come to my house and bring the box of evidence? ... Yeah? ... Great, I'll see you soon."

Rome set down his phone and gave Willa a reassuring smile.

It didn't take long for the newly appointed Sheriff to arrive; within almost 10 minutes he had rung the doorbell and graced the house with his presence, delivering everything they'd need from the police station.

"The new badge looks good on you, Charlie," Willa laughed.

"Why, thanks, love. But what happened to you?" his eyes filled with worry.

"Oh, not much, was just kidnapped by crazy people committing genocide," she deadpanned.

"Shit, that's what this is?" he frowned nervously.

"Yup," she sighed.

While Charlie and Willa made small talk, Rome had dug through the box and brought out the blueprints. He grabbed a highlighter from his desk drawer and began crossing off places he knew had been hit and messed with since they last were able to see it.

As Charlie looked over the new markings, he came to a realisation. "They're forming a pattern."

"What do you mean?" Rome asked.

"They're all going towards a back road – I know because I take that road with my wife when she has council events. It leads to the main Devonthorpe Tower. The building doesn't look like much now, but there are a ton of control systems that haven't been activated in years," he explained.

"But why would they hit there if it's so out of the way?" Rome asked.

"No, I get what you're saying… if they're linked, Annabel will flip a switch and surge everything in Devonthorpe, won't she?" Willa said, pointing to different targets on the sheet.

"Exactly, and they're within close proximity to shops or public areas along the way. With enough voltage, it's sure to travel and impact further than just the lines we see here," Charlie worried.

"So, this is where it's going to be, then?" Rome said the obvious out loud. "But when? Do we stake out there forever until they come? Because they'll find out one way or another and change their plan."

"You're right. It'll have to be an ambush, one we could achieve with Rosewood's help," Charlie said.

"I think I might know when," Willa said, trying to concentrate. When she was in the car, she heard a discussion between Annabel and the Commissioner about 'the big day'. But as she was going in and out of consciousness at the time, it was all unclear.

Willa concentrated, trying to recollect what happened next. She looked past the song on the radio at the time – all she had to do was interpret the buzzing of their voices.

"It's tomorrow," she suddenly recalled. "I watched her in the act today; she knew what she was doing, how elusive she was being. She was waiting for me to catch on, and if I didn't, she would've told me herself!"

"She was trying to protect you by telling you. She needed you to be on her team," Rome understood what Willa was saying.

"I'll never understand her attachment to me, but this friendly façade might just be the biggest slip up she'd made in her plan," Willa stated.

"Well, if it's tomorrow, I can find out when security expects people to use the tower. They hire it out for functions, so that's surely what Annabel would have done to get access," Charlie explained.

"Just make sure you don't give them a reason to suspect we're onto them…" Rome warned. "The security might be in on it, too."

"Understood, I'll be off then. I'll keep you updated," Charlie said.

"Thanks, boss," Rome smiled, giving respect to Charlie's new role.

Charlie chuckled at the thought until his face turned grim, and he headed out of the house.

"You should get out of town tomorrow, Willa. This isn't your responsibility, and if all goes wrong…" Rome began.

"Rome, I can't leave this now. I have to put a stop to Annabel as much as you do," she sighed, knowing the risks. Willa tried to stay calm, but her insides felt like they were melting at the idea that she might soon be a victim herself. "But I will call Poppy and tell her some lie to get her out of town; I feel like I owe her that much."

Rome looked at her, filled with courage as always. "You said that you'd never understand Annabel's attachment to you..." he began.

"Yeah?"

"But to me, it's clear as day, Willa. How couldn't someone be attached to you like that? I'd bend all the rules for you," he said honestly.

"Even if I were guilty like you thought?" she accused.

"Yes, actually. Even then. That's why I was worried," Rome gulped.

Willa smiled at his sincerity, although was somewhat unsettled by how easily he could be swayed. His responsibility was to bring justice to Devonthorpe, and she didn't want him to feel like he'd need to bury a body for her at the same time.

"I wouldn't put you in that position, Rome," she smiled, hoping her words were true.

Chapter Twenty-One

Willa sat up, wide awake because the day she'd been dreading had arrived. Yesterday, Charlie called to tell them that Annabel booked Devonthorpe Tower for 12:30pm, meaning they had the morning to prepare.

But for Willa, all she had to do was sit and wait. Rome had already left to liaise with Rosewood, and Charlie set up an action plan of his own. Once Willa convinced Poppy to skip town for some much-needed retail therapy at a warehouse sale, she had nothing left to do but mentally prepare herself.

Willa told Rome she'd be right by his side, trying to capitalise on her connection with Annabel. By all means, Annabel was beyond redemption. But if Willa could only convince Annabel that what she was doing was wrong, maybe lives would still be saved, even if Rome and Charlie's plan failed.

While Rome was hesitant about Willa being there, he realised the safest spot for her was by his side if things went wrong. At the control tower she wasn't at risk, it was the only place where people wouldn't be affected by the voltage.

But Willa didn't intend to be by Rome's side. She knew he wouldn't let her do things her way, so she had to go it alone. She learned the layout of the Devonthorpe Tower, knew where the control switches were, and that Annabel would be waiting for her there.

Willa looked at the time on an old phone and noticed the day was creeping up on her. She pulled her hair back, got dressed in dark clothes to match the tower's staff, and left the house.

***

Rome and Kathy were at a warehouse next door to the Devonthorpe Tower. It was 11:30am, and Rosewood officers began to file into the room one after the other. Everyone was set up in tactical gear for the mission.

After a while, Charlie arrived at the scene having sent his wife out of town. All reinforcements were there, but there was one face he didn't see.

"Don't make me say I told you so, Rome," Kathy said.

"Let's not go there again, Kathy," he answered before feeling his phone vibrate.

It was a text from Willa.

W: Rome, I'm so sorry, but I don't think I can be there after all. I'm skipping town with Poppy. I hope everything goes well.

Rome's chest went stiff, but he had to stay on task. He'd initially asked her to get out of town, and he can't blame her for doing just that.

In fact, without Kathy in his ear, he would be grateful to Willa because now he won't have to worry about her getting hurt. Yes, that's how he'd take it.

But he couldn't help but feel fragile about the contents of the message. It felt cold. Merely saying 'I hope everything goes well', what if it didn't? It was like she was disconnected and didn't care. Did his suspicion really hurt their relationship that much yesterday? He breathed out a steady breath and refocused on the mission.

"That's all of us now. It's time we go. Are we ready?" he asked.

"Yes, we're ready," Kathy answered for her team, choosing to hold her tongue in front of the others.

"You all know the drill. Let's roll out," Charlie piped in, and everyone split into their groups.

***

Willa had waltzed into the Devonthorpe Tower lobby, avoiding the gaze of the receptionist as she walked to the lighting room. She brought tool bag with her, as if she were here for maintenance work, and had a fitting excuse prepared just in case.

The lighting room was down two levels lower than the control room, and Willa learnt that there were hatches on that side of the tower leading from the bottom floor to the roof. Inside a cupboard on each level was a ladder, stored in case of emergencies when the elevator shuts down.

She went inside, grateful that her research was correct. If Annabel wanted the space to herself, the tower technicians couldn't be around. Willa ran to the corner of the room, jumping up and grabbing the hatch handle above her. She was confident that her plan would work. She opened the cupboard, pulled out the ladder and began to climb.

As she moved up the rungs, she saw Charlie down below through the window, acting inconspicuously. Their mission had also begun. She felt guilty about lying to Rome, but it had to be done.

She continued climbing, but as she reached the top, something grabbed her hand. Her eyes widened in fear as she looked up to see the cause. It was a strong man, that was obvious, as he lifted her up to the second level with no effort.

"What are you doing here?" he asked. At that moment, she recognised who he was – the driver who helped save her from Joe the day before.

212

"It's you," she was bewildered.

"You can't be here. It's private property," he said. Judging by his outfit, he was a security guard working at the tower.

"I'm doing some tech repairs," she answered, referring to her fake alibi, with a jingle of her tool bag.

"Tech support isn't here on Saturdays," he squinted his eyes. He'd caught her in the lie far quicker than she'd hoped.

"Look, I know; this, plus yesterday, it all seems really weird. I'm just a random stranger, but you have to trust me here," Willa started. "We're all in danger."

"Are you making a threat?" he asked.

"No, not from me! I'm the one trying to stop it. You saw me running yesterday," she answered, feeling irritated by the time he was wasting.

"But what are you doing here now?" he stood back, letting her go.

Willa peered down the window and saw that Charlie was still there with a few others. She knew she had to tell the guard some parts of the truth to get away.

"Someone here is about to do something *really* bad, and it might come to the point where I'm the only one who could stop them. I know you don't believe me, but just look downstairs. There's police ready to raid the tower," she said pointing.

He peered over and saw Charlie, who he recognised through his wife's frequent visits to the tower. She was telling the truth.

"What can you do about it?" he asked.

"Whatever I can," she sighed, knowing it didn't sound promising.

"...What can I do about it?" he said, gearing to her side.

"Let me go upstairs – then do whatever Charlie or Rome says when he comes inside," she said.

The man paused for a moment. "What was your name?"

"Willa Triston is my full name, if you feel you need to report it."

"Alright, Willa. Stay safe," he walked away, only to turn back. "But here, take this," he reached to his belt and detached his taser.

Willa took it cautiously, after which the guard finally left the room. She let out a breath of relief and refocused. Upwards and onwards she went.

***

Rome watched Annabel and Penelope exit a car, closely followed by a few others, talking happily with each other as they entered the tower. It made him feel sick. Seeing them so smug showed how easy this all was for them. Annabel honestly thought she was doing a service to the world with her revenge. But he had to wait, just a few moments more. When they raided, Rome needed the group to be inside properly, away from all the exits.

As planned, Kathy – the only one dressed in regular clothing, inconspicuous because she's not from the area – came out of the tower and scratched her nose.

It was the signal. Rome clutched his radio, shouting, "go, go!" The majority of the squadron harpooned themselves into the tower lobby, while some stayed behind to guard the surrounding exits.

"Police, everybody down!" Charlie ordered upon entry. The civilians dropped while the assailants began splitting up.

"John, what's going on?" Penelope shouted to the Commissioner.

"It's not me!" he yelled as they jumped behind the receptionist desk.

A security guard approached, and Rome worried that he would be on Annabel's side, ready for a fight.

"Stop where you are," Rome shouted, pointing his gun at the burly guard. He did as he was told, holding his hands in the air.

"Wait! My name is Rodger Briggs. I'm on your side. Willa said to do whatever you asked," he answered quickly.

Rome froze as he heard her name come from the stranger's mouth.

Somehow, Willa was looking out for him. He nodded and lowered his weapon. "Help shut off the exits."

He ran behind him. "On it."

Rome looked out, and his team had already begun rounding up some familiar faces, Florence and Xavier included. Still, the Commissioner was the only one armed.

Rome raced over to the front desk where he saw them hiding, but as he approached, shots were fired.

"Stay calm, stay down!" he shouted at the screaming public... but he felt like he was talking to himself at the same time.

"John, you traitor," Rome called out. "Put the gun down!"

"I'm the traitor? Look who's turning against me now," he shouted back.

"Shoot him, John!" Penelope hissed, only thinking of reclaiming her freedom.

"I don't have a shot," John fussed.

"Shoot him, or I will!"

Rome dove behind a pillar for cover, while John took another shot, to no avail.

"Damn it, give it here!" Penelope snapped, taking it for herself. She stood up out in the open, unphased by her vulnerable position. She aimed, ready to take a shot at Rome once more, and a gun fired loudly. But Penelope's scream proved it wasn't hers. Kathy shot Penelope in the arm, causing her to drop her weapon. She keeled over, cowering in pain and frustration. Rome ran over and kicked the gun away from John, who reached to grab it.

Rome pulled out his own gun and pointed it at the Commissioner, showing the victor. "Somebody, come and cuff them!" Rome shouted, and a young police officer from Rosewood followed his instruction.

John spat at the young officer, so Rome stepped forward and hit John with the back of his gun, knocking him out.

Rome looked down. "Disgusting."

He took a moment to assess how the bust had panned out, and thanks to their numbers, it was a clear win. The operation seemed to be under control, but there was one face he didn't see – Annabel's.

"Charlie, she'll be heading to the control room!" he shouted aloud to his friend.

"Rome, we've got another issue," he called out, prompting Rome to turn around.

Joe was standing at the door with a bunch of henchmen in masks. They were holding an array of weapons, from metal pipes, knives, and Joe's own gun.

"Shit," Rome said.

***

Willa heard gunshots from down below, and while she was worried, she couldn't let that distract her. She was too focused, trying to decipher the controls beneath her.

She couldn't disarm anything because she didn't even know what the buttons did. She was stuck, but she was in the right place, and she hoped that mattered.

She soon found it did matter, because as she'd feared, Annabel came charging into the room. She scurried inside with her heels held in her hand, which she would've taken off in the elevator. With the way she grasped the walls for support, Willa could tell she'd twisted her ankle in the altercation.

"Willa?" Annabel's mouth dropped as she saw her standing there.

"Annabel, this has to stop," Willa shouted across the room.

"No, Willa, you don't understand. This has to happen."

"Stay back, Annabel," Willa spat in detest.

"We were on the same page; you knew it yourself!" Annabel was wild, shouting at her for the first time.

"You need help," Willa said, almost giving her sympathy.

"No, no, this isn't about me, this is about everyone!" Annabel blurted as she hobbled over, fuelled by ambition.

"There's another way! There will always be another way!" Willa cried out.

"Why are you trying to save this place? What has it ever done for you? I've given you so many more opportunities!" Annabel became hysterical.

Gunshots fired again from downstairs, making Willa jolt.

"Do you hear that? That's not your precious Rome winning. That's us. We're going to make this happen because we know what it means if we don't. Whether it's today or tomorrow, it's inevitable!" Annabel said, drawing closer to the control panels.

"I said stay back—" Willa moved forward to block the way.

"You're not listening!" Annabel pulled out a compact gun from her dress pocket and pressed it directly against Willa's forehead.

Willa's breath hitched. "You don't want to do this, Annabel."

"You're right; I don't. But I will. I'll do it if you make me," she threatened. "So, move!"

"I can't do that," Willa said with courage.

"Yes, you can, just step aside!"

"No, I can't!" Willa said, pushing back, testing her luck.

Annabel's face grimaced – she didn't know what she wanted to do in this situation. It was easy to kill everyone when it wasn't by her direct hand, but this was different. It was her Willa, too.

"Please, Willa," Annabel begged.

The control room door burst open for a second time, and Rome appeared, relatively unharmed.

"W-Willa!" he stuttered.

His usual tanned skin turned ghostly pale when he absorbed the scene before his eyes. With a gun pressed to Willa's head and a strong chance of Annabel pulling the trigger, it was like he had stepped into his worst nightmare. Despite all of the ups and downs, Rome knew at that moment he'd do anything to stop her from getting hurt.

"Move, Willa!" Annabel pleaded urgently.

"Do what she says," Rome called out, fully aware of what would happen to the town if she did. Thrown off by Rome's unexpected stance, Annabel turned her head to face him. This gave Willa the window she needed to move out of the way.

When Annabel turned back, she saw Willa reach into her bag, grabbing the taser she'd been given. Willa quickly aimed it at Annabel, letting the charge release. As Annabel was falling, Rome watched her pull the trigger. The bullet missed Willa by an inch, but it showed her intent. There was no way the three of them were coming out alive. Now on the ground, Annabel steadied her hand, taking aim at Willa once more – Rome acted on impulse, drawing his weapon and firing first. It was finally over.

Willa looked down at Annabel as she bled out, knowing it was already too late for emergency help. She was dead. Beautifully resting – an image of the person Willa first met and adored.

They'd killed her, but Willa had to remind herself that it was all in self-defence... kill or be killed. At first Willa assumed Annabel would never hurt her, but her final actions showed how far she'd go for the cause. Rome ran over to Willa and kissed her as if his life depended on it... because, for a moment, it did.

"We're safe, Willa," Rome spoke, acknowledging the situation downstairs was also resolved.

"Thank goodness," she sighed. He held his arm around her waist, guiding her out of the room and away from Annabel's body.

"We have one casualty," he said to Charlie as they met upon exit.

"Are we good?" Charlie asked.

"We're good," he answered. Those simple words confirmed to Charlie that it was Annabel who died... and that Devonthorpe was saved as a result.

When they left the scene, Willa saw the aftermath of everything. Joe and his cronies were being loaded into the back of a police van, the Commissioner would be charged for corruption and attempted murder, and all of Annabel's allies were headed straight to the slammer.

Willa nodded gratefully at the guard, Rodger, before carrying on with Rome to his car.

"Hey, Rome! The paperwork!" Charlie called out to him.

"I don't work there, remember?" he said cheekily.

Charlie grinned and shook his head, mumbling a 'whatever' under his breath.

"You know you're going to be begging for your position back in no time, right?" Willa reminded him.

"Charlie couldn't stay mad at me, though Francine is another story," he laughed.

As they entered Rome's car, Willa's phone rang. It was Poppy.

"Hey, how did it go?" Willa asked.

"The sale was neat. I definitely scored some goodies. But Willa, are you alright? You said I had to call before I went home. Am I... able to come home?" Poppy asked. It was as if she knew there was more to the story.

"Yeah, it's all over now. You can come home," Willa took a breath of relief, feeling a heaviness leave her shoulders while Poppy hung up. And she was right. Their big adventure was over.

Rome started his car and began driving.

"Where are we going?" Willa asked.

"Somewhere I go to whenever I finish a big case," he said.

***

219

It wasn't long until they pulled up at an enormous field. Willa followed Rome's trail as they walked onto the grass, when he suddenly stopped in his tracks. He sat down on the ground and laid on his back.

"Uh, what are you doing?" Willa asked.

"Laying under the clouds is the perfect way to calm down after something like this, I promise," he said.

"Alright." She got down and snuggled up beside him.

They laid in silence for a while before Willa opened her mouth once more. "I guess this is the end for us, huh?"

"What?" Rome snapped to his side.

"Well, you know, we met because of this. Sure, we spent a lot of time together, but it was because of the case. Now that it's over, what will we do? You don't need me anymore," she joked.

But Rome wasn't taking it as a joke. The look of disbelief on his face was as clear as day. Moments back, when he almost lost Willa at the tower, he couldn't imagine life without her. Yet Willa thought he didn't need her anymore?

"Do you not understand how I feel about you?" he asked with sincere concern. She didn't respond, and instead waited for him to go on. It was his turn to make the next move. "Willa, I'm in love with you."

She rolled over, looking Rome in the eye. "I know."

"You know? Then why would you assume we'd end this?"

"I was just kidding, Rome."

He fell back, sighing as he steadied his heartbeat. Rome finally said all that he needed to, and she could take it how she liked. With everything they'd been through that day, he tried not to take her comedy personally.

"Hey, Rome?"

He sulked. "What?"

"Look at me."

He closed his eyes. "No."

He felt a weight press on his chest and opened his eyes to see Willa leaning over him. "I love you too, Rome."

He gulped. "You're serious, right?"

"As serious as ever," she said.

A grin took over his face as he rolled them both over, looking down at her. "I'm so glad we arrested you," he chuckled.

"Let's just not mention that part anymore," Willa cringed at their beginning.

"I love you," he said again, holding her face in his hands as they kissed in the sunlight.

In this moment of sweet bliss, Willa couldn't help but think how her life would change after today. The truth of the case would finally unravel, she would need to find a new mentor that wasn't involved in homicidal madness, and Rome would have to jump through hoops to get his job back. But they had each other's support, and Willa wholeheartedly knew they'd be alright.

The End.

About the Author

Elaelah Harley is an Australian author and editor working in the publishing industry. Her passion for literature started from a young age, writing short stories about her favourite childhood characters before taking on more original concepts.

Education consumed her early adulthood, achieving a Bachelor of Media and Communications from the Queensland University of Technology in 2018, then working in the field of journalism for over a year while studying a Graduate Diploma of Editing and Publishing through the University of Southern Queensland. She is currently working through her Master of Editing and Publishing.

Elaelah finds joy alongside her friends and family, spending time with her animals and getting swept away by a new book or TV series.

You can connect with her on:

- https://www.allwrittenthings.com
- https://twitter.com/ElaelahHarley
- https://www.facebook.com/elaelahbrookeharley
- https://www.instagram.com/elaelahharley

Made in the USA
Columbia, SC
02 December 2021